"A delightful, entertaining story of courage and perseverance in search for and acceptance of one's self."

Carolyn Seay O'Dell
Musician

"Easy reading with vivid imagery. Plays like a movie in your head."

Ron Jones
Educator

"This is great. It's the kind of story that you cannot put down until you have finished the last page. I would truly recommend this book for the greatest of pleasure in reading for all ages."

Margaret Thomas
Retired Postmaster

"Not only highly entertaining, but value based. This book is a reminder that if we find our God-given gifts, we can accomplish our dreams. A 'must read' for the entire family."

Reverend Eddie Willis

"Really terrific!"

Jane Klim Hughes
Bookstore owner

The Legend of
Auggie
the Awkward Elf

Frohe Weihnachten
Oma 2002

by Stacy A. Powell
with Diane Fuller

Illustrated by Dan Nagro

Best Wishes always,
Stacy A. Powell
Christmas
2001

Candle Fly Press
Spartanburg, South Carolina

Dedication

This book is dedicated to you, the children of the world. It is my hope that Auggie will help teach you to be responsible for your actions, to overcome misfortune, and to keep trying when things go wrong. Sometimes, hard times can make you stronger; and often, good times are just around the corner.

Remember, you are an individual, and in the whole world, there is only one of you. So take pride in yourself and in all the things you do.

Auggie, Robbie, and the whole gang at the North Pole wish you well; so do all of us at Candle Fly Press.

Stacy A. Powell
Author

Foreword

This is a family type Christmas story about the mishaps and misadventures of a young elf at the North Pole. It's all original and fast moving, from page one to a climactic ending.

This isn't your usual run-of-the-mill story. Auggie doesn't have magical powers or a fairy godmother to make his troubles disappear. No, I'm afraid Auggie has to deal with life's difficulties and his own shortcomings much like everyone else, although he has his own unique way of doing so.

Find out . . .
    . . . *Where elves live –*
    . . . *Things about reindeer you've never known before –*
    . . . *If all elves work for Santa –*
    . . . *How elves become Santa's helpers –*
    . . . *What the North Pole is really like –*
    . . . *How Santa makes his Christmas Eve journey.*

Get to know . . .
    . . . *Santa in day-to-day life at the North Pole –*
    . . . *The factory foremen –*
    . . . *Mrs. Claus like you've never known her before –*

The characters in my story . . .
    . . . *Auggie, the awkward elf –*
    . . . *Robbie, his best friend –*
    . . . *Tater, his food-loving friend –*
    . . . *Sherry, the infirmary nurse –*
    . . . *and many other loveable characters and toy factory co-workers.*

There hasn't been anything really new for Christmas in years; however, I don't think another Christmas will ever arrive without your remembering "The Legend of Auggie, the Awkward Elf." Why not make Auggie a part of your family Christmas tradition!

Stacy A. Powell

Chapter I

Auggie's Dilemma

Santa Claus stood by his window staring out at the heavy gray clouds of the North Pole. Already the snow was deep, and now it looked like more was on the way. Yet, winter was just beginning.

He glanced out over the toy factories and absentmindedly stroked his beard. They were behind in production because the early snow had closed the road and held up some of the supplies so badly needed for making the toys. Everyone was working overtime, because this year a lot of little boys and girls had been good - better than usual. They deserved their special gifts and must not be disappointed. He and all the elves would have to work long and very hard to meet demands. Production must go on and not be stopped for any reason!

At that very moment in toy factory #3, production was coming to a stop with a loud crash . . . bam . . . bam . . . tinkle . . . crunch. The conveyer belt slowly ground to a stop, while toy after toy fell off the end in a big pile. A little red fire truck teetered precariously on the edge. Simultaneously, elves came running from every part of the building to see what had happened. As they gathered around, there was a wiggle at the bottom of the pile. Laughter erupted when Augustus F. Elf, better known to his co-workers as "Auggie the Awkward Elf," slowly squirmed out from underneath the mass of toys.

Suddenly the laughter stopped and it was so quiet you could hear a pin drop - for there stood Mr. Otto, the plant foreman, looking down at Auggie. Just as he started to speak, the little red fire truck, still teetering on the edge of the conveyer belt, fell, shattering the silence. Mr. Otto slowly shook his head.

"Augustus, clean up this mess," he said, "and when you're finished, report to my office. The rest of you back to work, please!"

"Ye, ye, yes-s-s, sir," Auggie stammered, his face red with embarrassment. He scurried about picking up the toys, in his haste dropping more than he carried. He was soon covered with perspiration as he feverishly worked to clear away the mess he'd caused. It had happened so fast, he didn't know what went wrong. All of a sudden, he was on the bottom of the pile wondering if the toys would ever stop falling on him.

He was in big trouble - and he knew it - for this was the third time this month that production had come to a stop because of him.

Auggie remembered the first time he had stopped work at factory #3. He had been assigned to the toy robot division. His job was to attach the wires to the legs of the robots to make them walk. Things were going well for a while and he was so proud of himself. Here he was - Augustus F. Elf - the very first representative of the town of Littleburg, working for Santa Claus at the North Pole. His feeling of well-being and self-pride was short lived, however, for inspector #41 soon discovered that when you flipped the walk lever, the robots walked backward, not forward. It seemed that Auggie had crossed the wires. The robot division lost one and a half day's production due to his foul up.

Mr. Otto was very displeased. He scolded Auggie and said that since he could not put things together correctly, he would place Auggie where he wouldn't have to worry about him, and Auggie ended up in the marble department.

His job there was simple. All he had to do was load a dolly with eight large pails, each containing 4,000 marbles, roll them across the factory to the packaging machine, and pour the marbles into the hopper. They would come out the other end a few moments later in little plastic packages. It fascinated Auggie to watch the machine turn out the packs of marbles. Sometimes he thought of the children who would soon be playing with them in school yards all over the world, and it made him feel good to know he was a small part in bringing them some happiness at Christmas.

Auggie got along well with his co-workers and soon made many friends. He enjoyed watching the other elves put together all kinds of toys as he pushed his dolly across the plant. It was amazing the number of toys factory #3 could turn out in a day . . . and there were seven factories. He couldn't imagine that many children in the whole world. Even so, Santa said they were behind schedule and now they sometimes worked extra hours, but no one complained; for each elf knew the importance of his task, and like Auggie, was proud to be a part of the joy of Christmas. Things were going well, and he was regaining some of his self-confidence.

The morning of his thirteenth day in the marble department started out like any other. Auggie wove his way across the factory floor, pushing his fully loaded dolly. Robbie Elf, one of his new friends, called out a greeting from the catwalk above.

"Good morning, Auggie. Have a nice day."

Auggie looked up and waved. When he looked back down, his dolly was headed straight toward a big lathe. It was too late; he couldn't stop it. There was a loud bang as his dolly struck the lathe, and Auggie watched in anguish as the dolly, turning over seemingly in slow motion, sent 32,000 marbles scattering and rolling all across the factory.

Everywhere elves were falling and no one could stand up. If this had been a scene in a movie it would have been hilarious, but to Auggie, it was a nightmare. After a few minutes with everyone crawling around, the screaming and yelling settled down except for one voice and it was shouting, "Augustus!"

Auggie followed the sound of the voice and went around the corner. Mr. Otto was sitting on the floor, somewhat disheveled, his glasses askew. "Into my office, now," he said in a low frustrated voice.

Thank goodness no one was hurt, though they did lose the rest of the day's production gathering up the marbles. Unbelievably, all but one was accounted for. It was also Auggie's last day in the marble department.

The next day Auggie was reassigned to the end of a giant conveyer belt, and put on report for the second time.

Mr. Otto tried to be very patient as he explained to Auggie the duties he was to perform.

"As the toys come down the assembly line and are completed, they're placed on the conveyer and proceed to the end of the belt where you are to take the toys off, place them in cartons, and stack them for the inspectors to come by and pick up. Do you understand?"

Auggie nodded that he did.

"Good," Mr. Otto replied. He pointed to a control panel at one side of Auggie's station. "There are four clearly marked buttons here - Stop, Start, Slow, and Fast. Now, young man, Stop and Start are obvious. Slow is for a time when production is fast. You can slow down the belt so that you can catch each precious toy. Fast is for a slow time, so you can speed up the belt to get the toys quicker."

They went over and over the instructions until Auggie assured Mr. Otto that he understood.

Now four days later, as he picked up the last of the broken toys, Auggie realized what happened. Production was very good, so the conveyer belt was loaded down with toys endlessly coming down the line. Work as hard as he might, Auggie just couldn't keep up even though he rushed back and forth. I've got to work faster, he thought. As a big load of toys was coming down the belt, Auggie went to punch the Slow button, but he was thinking "work fast" - and Fast was the button he pushed. He immediately had been buried under a large pile of toys. It was a good thing the conveyer had an automatic shut-off; otherwise, there was no telling what might have happened.

After he finished cleaning up the mess he'd caused, Auggie went in to see Mr. Otto, who was seated behind his desk.

Mr. Otto looked up at him and slowly shook his head back and forth.

"Augustus, this is the third time that production has stopped because of you. This means you will have to report to Santa in person. I'm very sorry, but it's out of my hands now. There's nothing more I can do. You are to be in Santa's office tomorrow morning at seven o'clock; and whatever you do, don't be late because Santa is very busy."

Augustus, "into my office now!"

Chapter 2

Bad News

The bunkhouse was quiet as Auggie paced the floor. Robbie had been the only elf to speak to Auggie at supper. Auggie knew the other elves liked him and felt sorry for him, but he had caused them a lot of extra work, and they were all very tired and soon fell asleep.

Auggie continued pacing. "Oh me, oh my, oh me, oh my . . . I'm in big trouble!"

At 6:00 a.m. the next morning, the walls of the bunkhouse vibrated with the sound of the wake-up bell. Elves clamored out of their bunks. Some, like Robbie, very slowly, because Auggie's pacing and muttering had prevented them from getting a good night's sleep.

Auggie managed to pull himself up to a sitting position on the side of his bunk. It couldn't be six o'clock already . . . surely not; after pacing for hours, he had tossed and turned in his bed a long time before falling into a fitful sleep. It seemed like only moments before. Now tired and groggy, he just sat there in a stupor.

Tater Elf, another one of Auggie's few remaining friends, came running down the aisle and grabbed a coat off the bunk above Auggie. "Come on, we must hurry to the dining hall for breakfast," he said.

Tater got his nickname from his love of potatoes and food in general. He was not known to have missed a meal. Needless to say, Tater was a little overweight.

Soon the bunkhouse was empty except for Auggie. He staggered into the bathroom and washed his face. He just couldn't get his eyes open, so he stumbled back to his bunk and sat down on the edge. The big clock over the door read six-twenty. He would be too late for breakfast anyway, but by not going he would have a few extra minutes to get ready for his appointment with Santa. Oh, how he dreaded that. If only he could stretch out on the bunk for just a minute to get his thoughts together . . . OK, just for a minute.

Down at the dining hall Robbie was finishing off the last of his breakfast with one of Mrs. Fineworthy's honey biscuits. Mmm-m-m, how that lady elf could cook. She was a very special person and like a grandmother to all the elves. She always saw to it that everyone got all they needed, and sometimes, to Tater's advantage, a little extra. On special occasions she would reward them with some of her famous hot apple pies.

Robbie pushed himself away from the table and got up. Poor Auggie. He feared the worst. He looked around the dining hall for Auggie, but didn't see him anywhere. He did see Tater sitting at one of the front tables with Sherry, Pam, and Mandy. They were all co-workers and good friends, so he walked on over.

"Hi, girls."

"Hi, Robbie," they answered in unison.

"Tater, have you seen Auggie?"

Tater looked up and his eyes got big. "No, not since this morning. You mean he's not here?"

"What has Auggie got himself into now?" Sherry asked.

"I'm afraid he's in big trouble this time," Robbie said. "Help me look; we must find him."

They quickly checked the whole dining hall. But alas, no Auggie.

"What do we do now?" Tater asked.

"I'll go back to the bunkhouse and see if he's there," Robbie said.

"But there's not enough time. It's almost seven, and we must be at work in fifteen minutes." Tater said stuffing an extra honey biscuit in his pocket. "Besides, maybe he was too depressed to eat, and by now he's on his way to see Santa."

"I have to make sure," Robbie said.

"But you'll be late for work. Then you'll be in trouble too."

"Then I must get permission."

Tater's eyes widened.

Robbie looked toward the back of the dining hall where a platform ran the width of the room. It was used for special occasions and on one side was a large table where all the factory foremen sat. Each morning they ate breakfast, planned their work, and set their quotas for the day. Their meetings were not to be interrupted except for extreme emergencies.

"Thanks for your help girls," Robbie said. "I guess you'd better be off to work." He turned and headed for the big table.

Tater hesitated for a moment half listening to the girls' conversation while scanning the table for leftovers.

"Isn't Robbie handsome - and so brave!" Mandy cooed.

"I think Tater is kinda cute, too," Pam giggled.

"Come on girls," Sherry laughed. "We have to go."

Tater grinned at their remarks and then followed nervously after Robbie.

Robbie knew what he had to do. Auggie was his friend,

regardless of all the trouble and extra work he'd caused. Besides that, he felt somewhat responsible for the accident with the marbles. If only he hadn't distracted Auggie, this chain of events might not have happened.

He was now standing a few feet from the foremen's table with Tater fidgeting beside him.

"When the helicopter brings in the bearings today," Mr. Gustov, the foreman of factory #4 said, "we will be able to complete the roller-skate quota. Mr. Owen, I know you've been having supply problems at factory #6. How are things coming along now?"

"Well, we're behind on softballs, and we wanted to package the balls and bats together. But this week we began wrapping the bats separately, and when the softballs come in, we'll send them along."

Robbie cleared his throat loudly for a second time, hoping for someone's attention. He couldn't wait any longer, they were running out of time. When Mr. Owen stopped speaking, he swallowed hard and stepped forward.

"Sir, sir?"

Mr. Woodcock, the senior foreman stood and leaned across the table. "Yes, young man?"

"Sir, I'd like to report to Mr. Otto, please."

"I hope this is important." Mr. Woodcock said.

"It is, sir," Robbie answered, twisting his gloves in his hands.

Mr. Otto, who was sitting with this back to Robbie and Tater, turned. "What is it, Robbie?"

"In private . . . in private!" Robbie said.

"Oh; well, all right." Mr. Otto got up and the three of them walked over to the side. "What's this all about?" He looked at Robbie and Tater questioningly.

"It's Auggie, sir," Robbie said. "He didn't make it to the dining hall. He was up most of the night and we're afraid he's fallen back to sleep."

"What is to become of Augustus?" Mr. Otto wondered out loud.

"Please let us go check on him, sir," Robbie said. "He must report to Santa before it's too late."

"I don't know." Mr. Otto looked at his watch. "It's just a few minutes until work time, and Augustus has caused too many delays already."

"Oh, please, sir," Robbie insisted. "It wouldn't take long and we'll hurry!"

"No," Mr. Otto said.

Their heads dropped.

"Not the both of you. Just you Robbie, and you must hurry. If you're more than ten minutes late, I'll put you on report. Now be on your way, and you Tater, go straight to work."

"Yes sir, yes sir - thank you, sir," they flung over their shoulders as they ran out of the dining hall.

Outside, Robbie stopped and thought for a moment. He could make better time if he went up the alley behind the laundry, but he'd have to be careful for in back of the laundry were steam pipes that released excess pressure from the big boilers. This steam turned into a vapor which settled on the ground, melting the snow and causing a very large mud puddle with slippery ice all around the edges.

Off in the distance, Auggie heard someone calling his name. "Auggie! Auggie!"

"AUGGIE, WAKE UP! AUGGIE, WAKE UP!"

Then he felt himself being shaken. He forced his heavy

eyelids slowly open, and Robbie came into focus. He came awake with a start.

Robbie let go of his shoulders.

"It's five minutes until seven, Auggie, and you have to get dressed and report to Santa. Now, I've got to get to work or I'll be in trouble myself. Good luck, good friend," he said. Then he was gone.

Auggie jumped up and put on his dress coveralls. Grabbing his cap, he noticed the clock read two minutes until seven. He ran out the door and down the pathway as fast as he could.

Maybe Santa would be late. Maybe Santa would be held up. If he took a short cut down the alley between the dining hall and the laundry he could save a few minutes.

He cut down the snow covered alley-way and ran along at full speed. He had but one thing on his mind as he approached the laundry - and that was to get to Santa's office as quickly as possible.

Auggie came over a small rise and realized too late what lay in front of him. He felt his feet slip on the ice as he tried to come to a stop, and then it seemed he floated through the air for a moment before he hit the mud puddle face-first and slid all the way across to the other side on his belly.

Fortunately, he wasn't physically hurt. He pushed himself up and looked down at his dress coveralls. They were a muddy mess. A few minutes earlier they had looked so sharp. Now for the first time in his short adult life, Auggie felt like crying. There was no time to turn back and change clothes. He wiped the mud and the tears from his face, and with slumping shoulders, trudged on to Santa's office.

Standing in front of Santa twelve minutes late, Auggie wondered what he must look like. And, Santa, looking down past him to the muddy footprints across the carpet, no doubt wondered what ever had happened to this once eager elf.

"I - I - I can explain, sir," Auggie said.

"That won't be necessary, Augustus. Whatever happened to you this morning is of no consequence. The decision had to be made last night."

"Oh-h-h?" This didn't sound very good.

"They are forecasting a winter storm to hit this area late this afternoon. Our supply helicopter will be here at two o'clock today because it may be a while before it will be able to return. Augustus, I'm very sorry, but when the helicopter leaves today, you will have to be on it."

"Please, Santa, won't you reconsider?"

"Augustus," Santa said softly, "we don't make these decisions lightly. Mr. Otto and I met last night, and he spoke very well of you and how hard you try. Nevertheless, with the storm coming in we had to make an immediate decision. Your replacement will be arriving on the helicopter."

"But sir, isn't there something I could do . . . anything?"

"Even if there were something, Augustus, you would have no place to stay. Your bunk will be taken and there's no room to spare. Now I have work to do, and you will have time to say good-by to your friends and pack up. Maybe sometime you'll be able to return. Good luck to you, Augustus." With that, Santa left the room.

Auggie stood for a moment, then went out the door. It was a long walk back to the bunkhouse and the wind seemed colder . . . but he knew it had nothing to do with the oncoming storm.

Reporting to Santa

Chapter 3

Going Home

Auggie sat quietly on his bunk. Except for him, the bunkhouse was empty. He had packed his few belongings and gathered up his uniforms to turn in to the laundry when he left. He'd already washed the mud off his dress uniform the best he could. He would be ashamed to let anyone see it the way it was, and to guess what might have happened.

He sat there and thought about all the hard work, good times, and the friends he'd made at the North Pole. How was he going to explain to everyone back in Littleburg why he was returning? He was their first representative, and now he was a reject. Oh, he didn't want to go home . . . he just couldn't!

Soon it was lunch time and although he wasn't hungry, Auggie wanted to say good-by to his friends. He hated to go to lunch because by now everyone would know that he was leaving and it would be hard to face them; but it would be his last chance to see everyone. He left his bags on his bunk and apprehensively left for the dining hall.

Auggie found Robbie, Tater, Sherry, Pam, and Mandy all seated at the customary table. They exchanged greetings and Auggie sat down.

"Aren't you going to get something to eat?" Robbie asked.

"No, I'm not hungry. I guess you all know what happened."

"Yes," Sherry answered. Mr. Otto informed us this morning and we're all so very sorry, Auggie!"

"You have a lot of friends here that hate to see you leave," Pam added.

Auggie felt a hand on his shoulder and looked up. It was Mr. Otto.

"Augustus," he said, "it's not going to be the same around here without you, but you can make it back. Don't give up; keep on trying and one day we'll see you here again." With that, he gave Auggie's shoulder a squeeze and walked on.

"That's the kindest thing anyone has ever heard Mr. Otto say," Mandy whispered.

They sat there making small talk for a while. Occasionally, one of the other elves would walk by and pat Auggie on the shoulder. Some would stop and say a few words to him on their way out of the dining hall. It was almost time to go back to work. Back to work. Oh, how he wished he was going back to work.

Mrs. Fineworthy's voice broke into his thoughts. "Augustus, I saw that you weren't eating. Now, you must eat, so I packed you a good lunch because you have a long trip back home. I even packed you a little something special."

Auggie immediately thought of her apple pie. This was probably the last piece he would ever get. Tears welled up in his eyes and he stood up and hugged Mrs. Fineworthy for a moment.

"Now you take good care of yourself, Augustus," she said

as she turned and went toward the kitchen dabbing her eyes with the corner of her apron.

By this time, everyone at the table was standing. They were the last ones left in the dining hall and they, too, must get back to work. Robbie and Tater gave him big hugs. Pam and Mandy squeezed his hand, and Sherry leaned over and kissed him right on the cheek. Then they were gone. The large dining hall, which just a few moments before had been alive with the hum of voices, was now strangely silent and Auggie stood there all alone.

Back in the bunkhouse, he gathered his bags together and looked at his bunk. Tonight another elf would be lying there wondering if that large lump in the mattress above, which was Tater, would fall through on top of him. Auggie glanced around one last time and then left.

The wind was beginning to stir and snow was lightly falling as he entered the laundry. He placed his uniforms on the counter.

"Sorry, Auggie," Larry the laundry elf said.

Auggie only nodded his head and turned to leave.

"Wait, you get to keep your cap, and the way it looks outside you're going to need it."

"Thanks, Larry," Auggie said and walked outside. Larry was right; it looked like the storm was arriving early. The wind was gusting and the snow was falling heavier as he made his way to the Post Office. This was his next and last stop because the heliport was right on the other side. As if to punctuate his thoughts, he heard the helicopter hum overhead with its propellers beating in the snowy air.

Inside the post office, Auggie observed that the walls were lined with bags upon bags of mail to Santa. Children from around the world had written to tell Santa what they hoped for - but Auggie would no longer be a part of their Christmas.

"Auggie," Peter Elf the postmaster said, "I have one letter here for you. It's from Littleburg."

"Thanks, Peter."

"Good luck, Auggie," Peter replied softly.

Auggie walked outside and watched the helicopter land and saw his replacement get off. Auggie bore no malice toward this new elf, for he knew too well how hard it was to qualify to come to the North Pole and be one of Santa's helpers.

The wind was bitter cold now, so Auggie decided to step around to the sheltered side of the post office until the supplies were unloaded and taken to the warehouse. Oh, how he hated to go home, but it wouldn't be much longer.

On the helicopter things weren't going well at all. Frank was the pilot, and Joe was his crewman. Both were the "big people" as the elves referred to them.

"This is a rough one, Joe!"

"I know."

"How long to unload?"

"About half an hour," Joe replied thoughtfully, "twenty minutes at the least."

"There's no way we can take the supplies to the warehouse," Frank said. "This storm is really setting in. We'll be lucky to make it back to home base."

"Let's hurry," Joe urged. "I'll back the truck over."

"We can come back as soon as this blows over," Frank said. They quickly loaded supplies onto the truck and re-parked it. Then they climbed back aboard the helicopter.

"Weren't we supposed to pick up one of these little fellows and take him back with us?" Joe asked.

Frank scanned the cargo sheets.

"We sure were. Where is he?"

"I don't see anyone, but then I can't see anything except snow!"

"It's twenty after two," Frank said. "I thought he was sup-posed to be here at two."

"He was."

"We'll give him a couple of minutes while I start revving up the engine."

"I'll keep watch," Joe said.

Auggie was on the other side of the post office feeling sorry for himself and lost in his thoughts. Then he heard the helicopter revving up. OH, NO! He was jolted back to reality. Auggie grabbed up his duffel bag and ran around the corner toward the sound of the helicopter.

"See anyone?" Frank yelled to Joe.

"No," Joe shouted.

"We have to go."

"I agree."

Frank moved the throttle and the helicopter started to rise.

Auggie, running as fast as he could, heard the powerful engines going faster. As the helicopter came into view, it was already lifting up off the ground. Auggie hollered as loud as he could but they didn't hear him. In an instant, the helicopter was gone and Auggie was left standing in a swirl of snow and wind as the hum of the blades faded into the distance.

At this time of year - early November - the glow of the Northern Lights frequently lit up the North Pole, but today there was darkness because of the heavy clouds. The only light was in Santa's compound of factories, bunkhouses, and walkways. The lights would be on from 6:00 a.m. until 9:00 p.m.; then they would be turned off along with lights from any other area not in use.

Supplies were always short at the North Pole and conserving energy was a must. When Pete the Postman heard the helicopter churn off into the distance, he automatically turned and flipped off the heliport lights.

Auggie was still looking up into the snowy sky when the heliport was suddenly plunged into darkness. At first he was startled. He jerked around and looked back toward the Post Office. He could see Peter in the light behind the curtains. A momentary surge of relief swept through him as he realized that no one knew he was still there. After a few moments, the surge of relief was replaced by concern. Here he was at the North Pole, in the middle of winter, caught out in the open in the worst storm of the year. What was he to do?!

First, he had to get out of the weather before he froze or was discovered. Then he must think this situation through. By this time, Auggie was shivering and his options were few. That's when he thought of the truck - perfect! He could stay there until the lights went out. Then he would seek warm shelter.

It was difficult for Auggie to climb up on the running board and get the door open, for this was a big person's truck.

It was even more difficult to get his duffel bag pushed up and in, but he finally did and nearly fell out as he tried to close the door.

The wind and snow beat down, buffeting the truck, but he was safe for the time being. Auggie thought that it must be about three o'clock by now. That gave him six hours to decide what to do. Right now he was cold, so he got some extra clothing out of his duffel bag. He heard something hit the floor of the truck. He felt around and discovered that it was his scrapbook. He thought that looking through it would be a good way to pass the time, but he needed a light. He couldn't turn on the inside truck light because he was afraid someone might see it, so he dug down into his duffel bag and found his flashlight.

He opened the book and the first pictures were of his mom and dad, their home, and of himself as a baby elf. He sure was a funny looking baby, he thought.

There were other pictures of family and friends, and one of himself being christened "Augustus F. Elf." He was named Augustus for his grandfather, and the "F" stood for "Franklin" after the famous inventor and statesman, Benjamin Franklin. The story had been passed down that one of his ancestors built the kite that Ben Franklin used to discover electricity. He'd always been very proud of his name. Now he had dishonored it.

As Auggie continued to turn the pages, there were more pictures of friends and of his hometown, Littleburg. He turned another page and came to the pictures of his first Olympics. He smiled at some of them, for they were of friends from all over Elfland, and he would not forget them. Yet, all his thoughts were not pleasant and Auggie realized he was biting his lip. He had failed miserably in his first attempt at Santa's Olympics.

Wait! PLEASE WAIT!

Chapter 4

The Olympics

You had to be good to become one of Santa's Elves. You needed perseverance, the ability to work long and hard, and be able to assemble all kinds of toys (from bicycles to wagons) in a specified period of time. There were many tests of skill, dexterity, and endurance. Young elves from all over Elfland came to compete for the honor to serve Santa, and to represent their city at the North Pole. However, many returned home without realizing their dream, because each city was allowed only a certain number of representatives according to its size. In fact, Littleburg barely had enough population for one representative. Fortunately, Auggie was the only entrant.

Santa's Olympics lasted four days and was held in Capitol City. The first day was orientation. You received two packets of instructions: one in a big yellow envelope telling you where to sign up and what tests you were to take - and in what order. There was also a map of where you were to go and where you would be staying.

The second envelope was blue. In it were instructions of all the toys you would be expected to put together. You were to study these and prepare yourself for the first day of tests.

You were also allowed to visit the assembly rooms and see all the toys you would be working with in order to become familiar with them.

On his first day of testing, Auggie became so fascinated with the new toys he put together that he spent too much time trying them out and watching them work. Suddenly, the bell rang and he was far short of the production quota he needed to make in order to proceed further. So, after the very first day, he was on his way back home.

On his second try, Auggie did better. He kept his mind on the job at hand and learned that he qualified for the second day of tests. That night he took out his packets and studied very hard and very late. Finally, he sleepily put the instructions for the second day in his envelope and went to bed. The next day, Auggie was doing OK up until the final two hours of the afternoon class. Then he discovered that some of his instructions were missing. Apparently, he had placed them in the yellow envelope the night before.

At first he had panicked; but with grim determination he decided to continue, hoping he could figure out how to assemble the remaining toys. Unfortunately he failed to do so, and again, he was on his way home. One of the instructors, however, told him that he'd created some of the most unusual toys he had ever seen.

Auggie continued thumbing through his scrapbook and came to his third year try-out. Bittersweet memories crossed his mind because this had been his final try. The rules stated that each elf only had three tries in which to qualify. And if you failed the third time, you were out. Most would go back to their hometown and still be very happy and content to do their part by working in the factories that furnished supplies to the North Pole. But not Auggie. Nothing was more important than working for Santa.

On his third try, Auggie was still the only entrant from Littleburg, and he had prepared himself well. For most of the year he studied hard and worked in a little shop repairing broken toys. This time, with his previous Olympic experience, he was more at ease and even Lady Luck finally seemed to smile on him.

Auggie had been assigned a room-mate named Tommy. Tommy hoped to qualify for toy design school. His insight on how toys were put together and what made them work was truly a talent. He agreed to study with Auggie only after explaining with some difficulty that he had a speech impediment, and that he'd have to speak very slowly. Auggie told him that it was OK, because he learned slowly. They both laughed and studying together was never a problem. Tommy's help had been immeasurable and for the first time, when the Olympics started, Auggie felt confident.

The first two days went smoothly, and the second day he finished in the middle of the class. Things were going great! On the third day, Auggie continued to do well until that afternoon when he came to the final test - a 10-speed bike - oh, no! He had to assemble the bike in a certain amount of time. He could do it if he just stayed calm. He had trouble with these back at the repair shop and Mr. Peterson always helped him. Now Auggie was alone. He must work accurately and quickly. Beads of perspiration rolled down his face as he put the last safety reflector in place. There - it was done! Auggie picked it up from his work bench and set it on the floor. He was flushed with excitement; then he looked at his work bench. Lying there was one small piece about an inch long. Oh, NO! It was part of the brakes. How could he have missed it? He'd been so careful. He looked up at the clock and saw there were only three minutes left - not enough time. Oh me, oh my, failed again!

He picked up the piece, walked up to the instructor's desk and laid down the part, thus disqualifying himself.

Auggie stayed for the closing ceremonies and presentations, then attended the gala banquet. After all, this was his last time to be a contestant. The next time he came here, he would be a spectator. He congratulated the ones he knew who made it, and consoled some of his acquaintances who didn't. Most of those who didn't succeed would have another opportunity. For himself, he was through. He was feeling quite tired and ate very little.

Returning to his room, he found a note from Tommy on the dresser. It read:

Dear Auggie,

I PASSED! I PASSED! And I'm on my way home. I only have a few days before reporting to school and there is so much to do. I decided not to stay for the festivities. Sorry to have missed you - you're a great roommate.

Your friend,
Tommy

P.S. See you at the North Pole.

Auggie slowly crumpled the note in his hand. Oh, if only that were true.

The next morning Auggie was up early and on the train returning home. For most of the trip, he was lost in his thoughts wondering what he would do now. For the last three years, everything he did, his hopes and dreams, all had but one goal - to be one of Santa's helpers. Now that was over.

Mr. Peterson had said that Auggie could always work with him, and he liked Mr. Peterson. He was a good boss and treated Auggie fairly. In his depressed state, he couldn't make a decision so soon. Finally the train was pulling into Littleburg. Coming around a curve, Auggie could see the station platform up ahead. A lot of people were gathered on the platform and as the train pulled into the station, he could hear a band playing and people cheering. Auggie assumed there must be a big politician on board because it was close to election time in Elfland.

As he stepped down off the train, the band stopped and the people were momentarily quiet. Then they burst out with, "For he's a jolly good fellow . . . for he's a jolly good fellow . . ." It wasn't until he looked up and saw a banner that read, "Welcome Home Auggie - Our First Representative From Littleburg" that he realized this was all for him. Oh, no, there's been a mix-up. They think that I qualified. I must straighten this out because there's been a mistake!

Mayor Tweksburg, seeing Auggie's discomfort, rushed to him as everyone else crowded around.

"There's been a terrible mistake, Mayor," Auggie said.

"Oh yes, Auggie," Mayor Tweksburg replied. "There's

been a mistake all right, but it wasn't yours."

"W-w-what do you mean?"

"Quiet, everybody . . . quiet!" the mayor shouted. "Auggie doesn't know."

Laughter erupted all around. After a minute or two, the mayor raised his hand for quiet and everyone grew silent. Auggie was thoroughly confused by now and started to speak, but the mayor held up his finger.

"No, Auggie, let me explain. After the tests are over, veteran mechanics take apart the bicycles that are unfinished or defective. Upon dismantling your bike they could find nothing wrong. Puzzled, they double-checked to make certain they had the right bike. Checking again, they concluded nothing was wrong. The bike worked perfectly, so the instructor was called and he checked the bike. Then judges were summoned to convene at the test site. A determination was made that somehow an extra brake activator barrel was put into your test package. Further investigation showed you had finished on time - barely. They tried to reach you at your room this morning, but you had already left."

"Auggie," a familiar voice called. He turned and saw his mother, father, and Mr. Peterson, all beaming.

"Augustus," his father said, "what the mayor is trying to say is, you made it . . . YOU MADE IT!"

"We're all so proud of you, Auggie!" his mother exclaimed.

"Yes, we are," Mr. Peterson chimed in. "You're our first representative to the North Pole from Littleburg."

The band began playing and the people started cheering.

Two husky young fellows picked Auggie up on their shoulders . . . and in that moment, Auggie realized his dream had finally come true!

Oh no, time's running out!

Chapter 5

Fight for Survival

Auggie was lost in thought for a while; then he noticed that his flashlight was beginning to dim, so he put the scrapbook back and turned off the light to conserve the batteries.

It was then that he realized he was hungry - very hungry - for he had not eaten lunch. He felt around in the dark for the lunch bag Mrs. Fineworthy prepared for him. He found it and reached inside, wondering what she had fixed. As soon as he unwrapped the first sandwich he smiled, for he could smell it. He took a big bite - yes, it was - pimento cheese, his favorite!

Next, yea . . . his other favorite, peanut butter and jelly. Mrs. Fineworthy knew him well. He ate and thoroughly enjoyed himself. There was one parcel left in his bag. He took it out and smelled that familiar aroma. Sure enough, it was a piece of Mrs. Fineworthy's apple pie. He thought for a moment as he licked his lips; no, no, he must save this for later since he didn't know when he would be able to eat again. Thank goodness for Mrs. Fineworthy! If she were here, he'd give her a great big hug.

He sat in the darkness, listening to the wind as it rocked the truck. Periodically, he would stand up and rub his hands together and move around, trying to keep warm. Even with the extra clothing, he was still cold.

His situation wasn't good, but he had an idea. If he could find a place to stay out of the cold until the blizzard was over, the helicopter would come back and then he would get on board. He didn't want anyone to know that he even messed up going home. He wondered what Mr. Otto would think of that. Auggie could see him now, standing there and shaking his head and shouting, "Augustus!"

His plan was simple but sound - or so he thought. The only place he could stay was in the reindeer barn. It would be warm and he could hide there without anyone knowing. The only major problem was that the reindeer barn was all the way across the compound from the heliport. On a normal day it was a long walk, but in the darkness during a blizzard, it would be risky. There was no other choice; he must make it.

A little while later, as Auggie was looking out the window of the truck, he saw the lights start to go out, one section at a time, until the last one blinked off. It was unbelievably dark; there was no light from the moon or stars since the storm clouds blocked them out. The only lights left on at all were on the outside of each building. Occasionally, he could see one through the falling snow.

Again, Auggie went over his plan in his mind. First he would go to the post office, then to the laundry; there he could warm himself by the steam pipes that ran outside . . . on to the bunkhouses, then past the bunkhouses to the reindeer barn.

"I can do it," he said to himself, and with a deep breath he pushed open the door, shoved out his duffel bag (while forgetting his lunch sack) and jumped down to the ground. The wind slammed the door shut above him.

It took only a few seconds for the cold wind to cut through his clothes sending a chill up his back. In the cab of the truck, out of the wind, his body heat had knocked off some of the cold; but out here in the open wind, all warmth was instantly blown away.

Without hesitation, Auggie started in the direction of the post office. It was dark and the wind was hitting him in the face and eyes, so he plodded through the snow with his head down and his eyes partially closed. The force of the driven snow stung when it hit him in the face. Auggie trudged on. The snow was deeper now than when he entered the truck. He could feel it crunch under his feet. It was almost up to his knees.

With little trouble, he made it back to the post office and was pleasantly surprised to find that due to previous cleanups, the snow on the walkway was not as deep as it was on either side. That meant for the most part, he could conserve what little light was left in his flashlight because if he stepped off the walkway he could feel the snow get deeper, and he'd know to get back on again. Hoisting his duffel bag upon his back Auggie proceeded onward.

In a little while Auggie could see the light on the front of factory #6 off to his left, and soon he was passing factory #5. His nose felt like a cake of ice and his fingers were stiff, but soon, he thought, he could warm them on the steam pipes outside the laundry. The light from the laundry came into view and he struggled through the deep snow around to the side of the building. This was a warm place because the building shielded him from the wind, and the steam from the pipes swirled around.

Oh, it felt so good.

Auggie took off his mittens and put his cold hands on the pipes.

Ohhhh, ohhhh . . . that feels good, he thought. He could do nothing about his feet, however. There was no way to warm them. His fingers were regaining their feeling now, so he reached up and removed his hat in order to wipe the perspiration from his forehead. To his horror, Auggie realized it wasn't perspiration - it was water, and his hat was soaking wet. The swirling steam was settling on him. He felt his clothes and they were very damp, but not as bad as his hat. He had to get out of here fast or he was a goner. He wrung out his hat, put it on, and made it to the walkway heading in the direction of the bunkhouses.

Auggie knew his situation was perilous. In a matter of minutes his wet clothing would be frozen. The bitter wind was very cold and almost unbearable. His feet were so numb that he could no longer feel them, and he was forced to use his fading flashlight more and more often in order to stay on the walk. He was so tired – his icy clothing was much heavier and harder to walk in but he couldn't stop – for to stop was to freeze!

By the time Auggie got to the bunkhouses, he was no longer carrying the duffel bag; he was pulling it behind him through the snow. He couldn't go on like this. The duffel bag had to go, so he dragged it around to the side of his old bunkhouse and quickly covered it with snow. No one would see it there and he could retrieve it later.

Just a little farther . . .

He stumbled back to the walkway and stood there for a moment looking at the bunkhouse thinking how warm it was inside, and of his friends all curled up between their blankets, fast asleep. Auggie was so cold and tired. Oh, how he had tried to be like them; but no - he was Auggie - the awkward elf, and now he was on the outside looking in.

A gust of wind brought him back to his situation and he moved on, for there was still a long way to go. Auggie plodded on, staggering and sometimes falling. Each time he fell it was harder to get up than the time before. He fell again and knew he was off the path. He fumbled for his flashlight. The walkway was only a few feet to his right. He couldn't make it to his feet this time, so he crawled back to the walkway and continued toward the barn. Auggie slipped and fell on his side. Struggling to right himself, he looked up and couldn't believe it! He could see the light on the front of the barn. A surge of excitement raced through his body and he clamored to his feet and rushed to the barn door. His heart was beating fast. He'd made it! He'd made it! Soon he would be warm; soon he would be dry! He was safe! His hand reached the door handle - he was safe - the handle turned and the door opened a crack. He was saf_!? Light spilled out from the cracked doorway and he heard voices coming from within.

Auggie stood by the door, almost paralyzed with cold and fear. Just a matter of a few inches and he would be warm, but he recognized the voices and dared not enter. One of the voices belonged to Mr. Olaf, the stablemaster, and the other belonged to Santa Claus. Although the wind was howling, Auggie listened intently and could tell that Donner had come in contact with a pitchfork that had been left out and she had hurt her leg. Mr. Olaf was very upset and was blaming himself for the accident.

"There, there, Mr. Olaf; accidents do happen," Santa consoled.

"Not like this," Mr. Olaf retorted. "If I'd only remembered to put the pitchfork back in its place, this would not have happened. I'm too old and should have retired long ago."

"But we needed you. And, you stayed at my request. Now don't fret about it any more, Mr. Olaf. You're the best and the reindeer love you."

"I love them, too, Santa."

"Will she be able to make the journey Christmas Eve?"

"I don't think it's too bad, if it doesn't get infected."

"Great!" Santa exclaimed. "She's a good reindeer."

"I'm planning to stay with her tonight and I'll keep her calm and make sure the bandage stays on."

These words struck Auggie like a sledge hammer. Mr. Olaf was spending the night in the barn!

"Well, I hope you both get some sleep, Mr. Olaf. Keep me posted on her condition."

"Yes, sir," Mr. Olaf sighed.

Auggie jumped back from the door and hid at the side of the barn while Santa passed, and then watched until his flashlight beam disappeared down the walkway. The first excited rush left Auggie and the cold returned. He stood there leaning against the side of the barn - his little body shaking. He was spent and there was no place to go. He should give up and just walk into the barn and tell Mr. Olaf. He would be fed, given warm dry clothing, and he would have a place to spend the night out of this storm. Then he thought of all the commotion it would cause. Everyone would probably get up, and in the morning at breakfast they would all know that Auggie had done it again. He found himself wishing he were one of the reindeer, with Mr. Olaf's loving hands taking care of him.

No - he must find a place to stay. On the other side of the barn, Auggie remembered, was the tack room. It was a small building that housed the sleigh Santa used, along with all the bridles, reins, and extra runners. Yes, he could stay there. The little building had no heat, but at least he would be out of the storm. He struggled around the barn toward the tack room. Going inside, he turned on his flashlight and looked around. It felt good to be in out of the wind. The sleigh was parked in the middle of the floor and had a canvas over it. Auggie climbed up, drew back the heavy cover, and got in. He pulled the canvas around himself trying to keep warm. He was so sleepy, having had very little sleep the night before. It was really catching up with him now that he had stopped.

Auggie knew he shouldn't go to sleep in this cold, unheated room. He must sit up, walk around, and stay busy in order to keep warm. He pulled off his mittens and started rubbing his hands together. He heard the rustle of paper. He stopped and reached inside his coat pocket and pulled out his letter. Auggie had forgotten all about it. He leaned back, turned on his flashlight, and started reading. It was from his mom.

Dear Augustus,

I received your last letter and was glad to know that you were doing so well in the marble department.

Auggie flushed, for he had not written about his difficulties at work since then. They all thought he was still doing well. The letter continued -

Your father and I miss you terribly Augustus, but we're very proud of you and are happy that you are doing what you wanted to do for so long. Everyone here is excited about finally having a representative of Littleburg at the North Pole. The City Council met the other night and decided to have a plaque with your name on it placed at the entrance to City Hall.

When you come home for summer break, Mayor Tweksburg is planning a parade and a picnic at the City Park. Mr. Peterson comes by and reads your letters. He and your dad send their love.

I'll close for now, Augustus. I know it's getting close to Christmas and you must be very busy, or you would have written. Send us a letter when you can.

Love,
Mom

Tears began falling on the letter, and Auggie cried long and hard. Oh, how could he go home now, he thought as exhaustion overtook him and he passed out.

Inside the barn, Donner was lying in the hay on the floor. Mr. Olaf checked Donner's bandage again, then sat down in the stall and leaned back against the wall. He picked up her head and placed it in his lap. She looked up at him with big loving eyes.

"Don't worry girl," he said. "I'll be here with you all night and you're going to be just fine." Little did Mr. Olaf know that his great love of the reindeer could prove to be fatal for Auggie.

Hiding from Santa

Chapter 6

Auggie is Missing

The storm raged through the night, but by early morning it had passed.

At Santa's house, Mrs. Claus - or Mother Claus as all the elves referred to her - was in the kitchen preparing breakfast. She noticed the wind had died down and was glad that the storm was over. She heard Santa rustling around getting dressed and she smiled. How could he be so quiet going down a chimney when he made so much noise at home?

Soon all the lights would come on and she and Santa would sit by the window eating breakfast, watching the elves as they scurried to the dining hall and on to work.

This was her favorite time of the day. It was about the only time she and Santa had to share and relax, for he had much work to do, maps to study, and plans to finalize. Then she heard the radio come on in Santa's office.

"Helicopter base to Santa Claus, helicopter base to Santa Claus, come in . . . come in."

She glanced at the clock on the kitchen wall; it was 5:30 a.m.

"Oh, dear, oh, dear," she said.

Except in an emergency no calls came in or were accepted before breakfast. Something was wrong. She was closest to the radio, so she hurried into the office and picked up the mike.

"This is Santa base . . . come in . . ."

"Mrs. Claus, this is Frank, and I hate to disturb you, but I need to check with Santa on something."

"Here he comes now, Frank . . . stand by."

"It's Frank, dear. There seems to be a problem."

Santa mashed the mike button. "Frank, this is Santa. Do we have a problem?"

"Santa, I'm sorry to disturb you, but I don't know if we have a problem or not. We were supposed to pick up one of your elves yesterday; however, when we were forced to leave a little early he was nowhere to be seen, and we couldn't wait any longer because of the approaching storm."

"You mean no one boarded the helicopter?"

"Yes, sir. We didn't think that much of it then, but I got to worrying about it last night and decided to call you first thing."

"You did right, Frank. I'm sure there's an explanation. I'll check into it right away."

"The weather is clearing here, so we'll be in this morning with another load of supplies. We'll deliver them and take the truckload we brought yesterday up to the warehouse for you."

"That's good, Frank. We need those supplies. Thanks for calling - Santa base out."

"Helicopter base out."

Santa rubbed his head and almost smiled. "That Augustus. He missed the helicopter."

"Isn't that the one you had to send home?" Mother Claus asked.

"Yes, and I hope he hasn't done something foolish. I'm hoping he stayed with some of his friends."

Santa looked out the window and saw all the lights were on. It would be impossible to check on the elves now. Some were already on their way to the dining hall. He'd have to wait until they were all there, and then go look for Augustus.

Mother Claus noticed the deep concern on Santa's face as they ate a hurried breakfast. She knew he was hoping, as she was, that this little troubled elf was safe.

Although the storm was over, a bitter cold wind still blew outside. The dining hall was full and abuzz with chatter. It was warm and cozy as always and the aroma of hot honey biscuits raised everyone's spirits.

Robbie always liked to spend a few minutes here before starting the long workday. Then the door opened and he saw Santa walk in. At first only a few noticed, but as Santa walked from table to table looking up and down each one, a hush fell over the dining room. It wasn't unusual for Santa and Mrs. Claus to come for supper, but was very unusual for either of them to come to breakfast, and it was obvious that Santa was NOT there to eat.

After going around to each table, Santa went to the big table where all the plant foremen sat. He said something to Mr. Otto and then went into the dining hall office behind the table. Mr. Otto stood up and looked around, his face grim. Then he came down and headed straight to the table where Robbie was sitting with Tater, Sherry, Pam and Mandy.

Mr. Otto walked up and said firmly, "Robbie, would you and Tater follow me, please."

Robbie and Tater followed Mr. Otto to his office. They were completely puzzled by this turn of events. Santa was seated behind the desk as they entered, and he looked up as Mr. Otto closed the door behind them.

"Gentlemen, Mr. Otto tells me you are Augustus' best friends," Santa said. "While I admire close friendships, there is a very important question I have to ask you, and it's something I must know immediately."

"Yes, sir . . . yes sir!"

"Augustus did not get on the helicopter yesterday, and I need to know if he spent the night with you, or do either of you know his whereabouts?"

A look of astonishment and anguish crossed their faces and their mouths fell open as they tried to speak.

"No need to respond; I can see my answer," Santa said with despair in his voice. "I was afraid of that - you may return to your seats."

All eyes were on them as Robbie and Tater returned to their table.

When they sat down, Sherry whispered, "What's going on?"

Pam and Mandy leaned forward as Robbie spoke.

"Auggie missed the helicopter and no one has seen him."

Sherry paled. Her nursing experience told her that no one could have survived last night without a warm place to stay. Pam and Mandy wiped tears from their eyes. The office door opened and Mr. Otto and Santa came out.

Mr. Otto stood aside as Santa walked to the front of the platform.

"May I have your attention, please?"

You could have heard a pin drop in the usually noisy dining hall.

"We have a dire emergency," Santa said. "It seems that Augustus F. Elf, better known to most of you as 'Auggie,' has been missing since yesterday afternoon."

Santa heard a gasp and turned to see Mrs. Fineworthy, who was standing by the kitchen door, collapse to the floor in a faint. Mr. Fineworthy and several of the ladies in the kitchen rushed to her aid. The whole dining hall was a hubbub of concern and shock. After a moment, Santa raised his hands and everyone quieted down.

"I know that the conditions outside are still extreme, but I must ask for volunteers to search for Augustus. Anyone who wants to volunteer, please stand up."

Santa was startled . . . for the sound was thunderous as EVERY elf - the foremen included - jumped to their feet!

Santa stood there for a few moments overcome by the outpouring of love these elves had for each other. He was glad he lived at the North Pole - if only all the people of the world could be like this, then Christmas would be every day.

He raised his arms again for quiet.

"I know all of you would like to find Augustus, but too many looking may impede the search and could possibly destroy any clues that may be left. I'm putting Mr. Otto in charge of the search party, and each plant foreman will send two volunteers to report to him. Now, I've been told that Augustus was here yesterday at lunch time. Did anyone see him after that?"

"Sir!" Larry from the laundry stood up.

"Yes, Larry?"

"He came by and turned in his uniform, except for his hat. He only stayed a minute and then left."

"Anyone else?"

Pete the postman stood. "He came by on his way to the helicopter and picked up his mail. He had a letter."

"Did he say anything that would make either of you think he might not board the helicopter?" Santa looked at them hopefully.

"No, sir, he just looked depressed and said very little," Larry replied.

"Same story here, sir," Pete agreed. "I didn't see him after he left. I thought he was on his way home."

"Very well," Santa said. "Now we all must get to work. The ones chosen for the rescue team, please report to Mr. Otto at Plant #3 as soon as possible. We'll keep the rest of you informed as soon as we know something."

Emergency Call

Chapter 7

Let's Find Auggie

The rescuers assembled at Plant #3 and Mr. Otto saw to it that they were well equipped with snowshoes and rescue equipment. He chose Robbie and Tater as the two search team members from his plant.

"Robbie, I chose you and Tater because you are his best friends and you know him better than anyone, so I want the two of you to go out on your own and try to think like him. Maybe you'll get lucky. The rest of us will systematically search every square foot of the compound."

Turning to the group he said, "Gentlemen, the storm is over but the cold front is still with us. The wind is dying and it's way below zero. Augustus is out there somewhere and his chances are not good. Every minute counts; be careful and be sharp. Now, "LET'S FIND AUGGIE!"

Outside, the rescuers dispersed according to Mr. Otto's instructions. Robbie rubbed his chin and looked at Tater. "We have to have a plan."

Tater thought for a moment. "Why don't we start at the last place he was seen?"

"That's a very good idea, Tater."

And off they went. After looking around the post office, they went inside and talked to Pete. He could add nothing to what he'd said at the dining hall. While they were talking, the helicopter passed overhead and landed at the heliport.

Leaving the post office, Robbie saw Joe and Frank climbing down out of the helicopter.

"Let's go over and talk to them, Tater. Maybe they can tell us something new."

Joe and Frank were concerned too, but could shed no light on Auggie's disappearance. Frustrated in their efforts, Robbie and Tater turned to leave.

Joe stepped up on the running board of the truck and opened the door. "Hey, Frank," he yelled, "I'll take this load to the warehouse and bring you back a cup of coffee before we unload the . . the . . ." He saw a brown paper bag on the seat of the truck. He grabbed it and shouted to Robbie and Tater, "Hey, . . . hey, you two!"

They turned around and Joe held up the sack. "Say, did either of you little fellows leave your lunch in the truck?"

Robbie and Tater looked at each other.

Could it be?

They ran back to Joe. Robbie took the lunch sack, opened it, and pulled out a frozen piece of Mrs. Fineworthy's apple pie.

"It's Auggie's!"

"Are you sure?" Joe asked.

"We haven't had apple pie in a week."

"I know," Tater moaned.

"Don't you see, " Robbie said, "she packed a lunch yesterday for his trip, and you know she would've put something special in it for Auggie."

"Say, you're right!" Tater said.

"He must have spent the night in the truck, but he's not there now." Robbie's voice was rising with excitement. "That means he made it through the night and he's around here somewhere."

"Yes!" Tater exclaimed. His voice, too, was filled with glee.

They started to jump with joy, then Frank stepped up.

"Easy boys . . . we still have a problem."

"What? Auggie's all right, isn't he?"

"I hope so," Frank said, "but he didn't spend the night in the truck. If you look, you'll see that ours are the only footprints around the truck this morning. Auggie would have left footprints, too."

"Oh." Robbie raced around to the other side of the truck, but Frank was right. No footprints!

"Where could he have gone?" Tater asked.

Robbie looked around. "Maybe he tried to make it to the bunkhouse."

Robbie handed the lunch sack to Tater and he stuck it in his coat pocket.

Frank walked over. "We have a little extra fuel in the helicopter. While Joe's unloading the truck, I'll take it up and have a look around. Maybe I'll be able to see something from up there."

"Thanks," Robbie said. "Tater, let's go."

They headed for the walkway to the bunkhouse. When they reached the place where the main walkway split and went up in front of the bunkhouses, Robbie suddenly stopped.

"Wait!"

"What?"

"We have to part here. You go up the main sidewalk and

I'll take the shortcut because we don't know which way he might have gone."

"I guess you're right. I'll meet you on the other side of the laundry."

Walking along, searching for clues, Robbie wondered how anyone could've survived last night in the storm without proper gear. It was very cold now and it was even worse last night. Maybe Tater was having some luck.

Tater was well on his way, carefully looking all around as he went. His hands were getting numb, so he put them in his coat pockets to keep them warm . . . and he felt the lunch sack. His mouth watered and a stab of hunger hit his stomach. It had been a long time since he ate any of Mrs. Fineworthy's apple pie.

Auggie wouldn't mind, he thought. No - that wouldn't be right. After a few more minutes he reasoned, well, if Auggie were here he'd share it with me, so I'll just eat a little bit of it.

Robbie approached the rear of the laundry, and saw several elves there with Mr. Otto and they seemed rather excited. Robbie ran over.

"What is it? What is it?"

Mr. Otto explained, "The steam kept the snow from settling here and we found some icy footprints and signs that someone came this way last night."

"He probably came here to get warm," Robbie said.

"I hope he didn't stay long." Mr. Otto's face was grim.

Robbie felt the mist then and knew what Mr. Otto meant. They all walked over away from the mist and Robbie reported what he had found and that he and Tater were following their hunch about the bunkhouse.

"Well, you and Tater keep looking. In the meantime, we

will stick to our plan. If you find anything, signal us," Mr. Otto instructed.

"Yes, sir, we will."

Robbie started up the walk and was met by Tater.

"Find anything?"

"No, not a sign."

Robbie explained what had happened behind the laundry. By this time they were approaching their bunkhouse and heard the helicopter overhead. Robbie smiled. These big people were good guys.

Tater nodded toward the bunkhouse. "Do you think he's hiding inside?"

"Well, he wasn't there this morning," Robbie said, "but let's have a look." Hoping against hope, they entered the bunkhouse. Even after a thorough search, there was still no sign of Auggie. They went back outside and were trying to figure out what to do next, for they had reached a dead end. What to do?

"LOOK!" Tater shouted.

Robbie turned and looked the way Tater was pointing. It appeared that something had been dragged or that someone had crawled around the corner of the bunkhouse, and even though snow had fallen, there was still a faint indentation.

They ran as they followed the trail, stumbling around the corner, and then stopped dead in their tracks . . . gasping . . . because the trail led about halfway along the side of the bunkhouse, stopping at a big lump covered with snow.

Quickly Robbie regained his composure and rushed up to the mound and dropped to his knees beside it. Tater followed and stood behind Robbie. Robbie was having trouble raising his hands to remove the snow because he was so afraid of what he would find. Tater turned his head.

"I can't look."

Robbie reached out and brushed the snow away. Letting out a sigh of relief, he whispered, "Thank goodness!"

Tater turned around and looked down. It was something brown . . . it was Auggie's duffel bag. Robbie picked up the duffel bag and they walked back out to the walkway.

"If he was here, why didn't he come into the bunkhouse to be safe and warm!" Tater said.

"And why would he leave his duffel bag?"

"Maybe it was too heavy and he left it there," Tater replied.

Robbie stood there thinking about Tater's last statement.

"You might be right. You may have something there."

"I . . . I have?"

"Yes. Don't you see? If Auggie stashed his duffel bag there, then he intended to come back and get it. He covered it well with snow to conceal it because he didn't want us to know he was still here!"

"Why would he do that?"

"Who knows how Auggie thinks," Robbie said. "But we do know one thing; Auggie had a plan, and now we have to figure out what it was."

"How?" Tater asked.

"We start at the beginning." Robbie knelt and drew a line in the snow. "Let's see - from the heliport he went to the laundry and on to the bunkhouse, but didn't go in."

"Yet, he hid his duffel bag," Tater said.

"Right, because he was tired and it was too heavy to keep carrying."

"That means if it was too heavy to carry on, then he had further to go."

"You're absolutely right, Tater." Turning, Robbie looked past the bunkhouses. The outline of the barn caught his eye. He leapt to his feet, grabbed Tater by the shoulders and began shaking him. "I've got it . . . I've got it!" he shouted.

Tater looked startled. "Got . . . got what?"

"I know where Auggie went!"

"You do?" Where . . . where?"

"Go get Mr. Otto and the others. Tell them to meet me at the barn! Run - quickly!" Robbie shoved Tater on his way. Then he turned, kicked off his snowshoes, and raced toward the barn.

Mr. Olaf jumped back in surprise when Robbie came bursting through the door shouting, "Auggie, Auggie!" His voice was shrill with excitement and he went racing around looking in each stall and startling the reindeer.

"Here, here," Mr. Olaf said sternly. "What's going on?"

Robbie rushed over to him. "It's Auggie, sir. Auggie's here. This is where he spent the night, and now he's hiding."

"That can't be, son, for . . ."

"Oh, yes, sir. He just has to be here." Robbie hurried to the ladder and quickly climbed up into the hay loft. "Auggie, Auggie, come out. Please come out, Auggie," he called as he tore into the stacks of hay. But Auggie didn't come out. He wasn't anywhere to be found.

Drained of energy from all the frantic searching, Robbie slowly walked to the front edge of the hay loft and looked down. Below, looking up at him were Mr. Olaf, Mr. Otto, Tater, and the rest of the rescuers.

"He's not here, sir," Robbie sighed. "I . . . I was so sure. He came in this direction and the barn was the only warm place to stay and not be noticed."

"Tater explained what you found," Mr. Otto said, "and I can follow your line of thinking, Robbie."

"But," Mr. Olaf interrupted, "if he was planning to stay here undetected last night, he would've had to change his plans."

"Why, sir?"

"As I tried to tell you before, Donner hurt her leg yesterday and I spent the night with her, here in the barn. To my knowledge, Santa was the only other person to come by."

"That means he spent the night out there in the cold somewhere."

"I'm afraid so, son."

Robbie made his way to the ladder, came down, and apologized to Mr. Olaf for upsetting the reindeer.

"That's all right this time," he said. "You were only trying to help a friend."

Not wanting to disturb the reindeer further, the rescuers reassembled outside the barn. Mr. Otto turned to Robbie. "Though your idea was a good one, we've lost valuable time. We must get back to our systematic search. You and Tater follow your noses, but don't interrupt us again unless you find him."

"Yes, sir."

Mr. Otto and the others started back down the walkway.

"Here," Tater said, and handed Robbie the snowshoes he had kicked off earlier during his race to the barn.

"Thanks for bringing them."

"You're very welcome."

"I believe Auggie is close by," Robbie said. "I don't think he could have gone much further."

"Really?"

"Yes."

Then Tater hollered at the top of his voice, "A-U-G-G-I-E . . . AUGGIE . . . WHERE ARE YOU?"

Chapter 8

Race Against Time

Inside the tack room, Auggie came momentarily awake. Was, was that voices he heard? Was someone calling his name? He tried to sit up, but couldn't move. He was too weak and his clothes were almost frozen stiff. He tried to yell but could only manage an inaudible croak.

Auggie could no longer feel the cold. He could hardly think. He felt himself slipping away. He had to fight it. To slip away again, Auggie knew, would mean death. Somehow, if someone was looking for him, he must let them know he was in here. THE FLASHLIGHT! He wondered if it would still work. If he could just turn it on, maybe someone would see it. It was his only chance. He tried to move his arm, but couldn't. He felt himself slipping again, and the feeling was good. He just wanted to go to sleep. Sleep . . . beautiful s-l-e-e-p.

NO! A voice from deep inside seemed to shout at him. Don't give up. Try . . . try one more time! Auggie was fading fast, but with the last drop of willpower he could muster, he pushed his thumb with all his might. A faint click was the last thing Auggie heard as he lost consciousness.

Outside the tack room, Tater yelled a few more times.

"Do you think it helps to call him?"

"It couldn't hurt," Robbie said, as he took a few steps over to the tack room. "I don't know, though, if Auggie would be able to answer."

Robbie leaned against the side of the building and bent over to put on his snowshoes.

"What the . . . what was that?" he said. For as he bent over, his head had passed by the window and something caught his eye. He looked up through the window and there was a light - a circle of light on the ceiling! He quickly brushed away the snow from the window and peered in. It was a very weak light, but no doubt about it, it was the glow of a flashlight. Although Robbie couldn't see him, he knew it had to be Auggie.

Turning to Tater, who was watching the others go down the walkway, he yelled, "Tater, go bring Mr. Otto."

Tater hesitated, "What . . . what did you say?"

"We've found Auggie! Get Mr. Otto!"

"I hope you're right this time." Tater raced off after Mr. Otto as Robbie ran to the door and flung it open and turned on the light. At first he didn't see Auggie. Then he saw the canvas bundled in the seat of the sleigh. A little hand was protruding from under the canvas and it held the weakly burning flashlight. Robbie hurried over and threw off the cover.

"Auggie . . . Auggie!" he cried. Auggie did not answer. Robbie grabbed his foot and tugged at it. The flashlight fell to the floor of the sleigh. Still, Auggie did not answer.

Approaching footsteps got Robbie's attention and he turned as Mr. Otto, Tater, and the other rescuers entered.

"He's over here, sir." Robbie's shoulders sagged and he choked back a sob. "But I'm afraid we're too late." Mr. Otto quickly climbed into the sleigh beside Auggie. The rescuers held their breath as they anxiously waited.

Mr. Otto tore open Auggie's coat and layered shirts at the collar. Ice particles fell away from his frozen clothes. "Oh, Augustus, you poor little awkward elf. What have you done?" His heart was in his throat and his voice barely audible. "I hope we found you in time!"

Mr. Otto took off his gloves and put his hands inside on Auggie's chest, but they were numb with cold and could feel nothing. He pulled his hands out and blew his breath on them and rubbed them together to warm them. As he put his hands back inside Auggie's shirt, Auggie's eyes opened and for the briefest instant, he looked up at Mr. Otto. Then his eyes closed.

"He's alive!" Mr. Otto shouted. "Quick, bring me a blanket!" The blanket appeared almost instantly and Mr. Otto wrapped it snugly around Auggie and picked him up in his strong arms.

"I'll go get the rescue sled," volunteered one of the elves as they came out the door.

"There's no time," Mr. Otto answered. And with tears streaming down his rugged old face, he carried Auggie every step of the way to the infirmary.

Robbie raced ahead of Mr. Otto to the infirmary and ran in the door. Sherry was sitting behind the nurses' station and looked up expectantly.

"We found him! Mr. Otto is bringing him - he's alive!" Robbie blurted out.

About this time, Tater came through the door and held it open as Mr. Otto brought Auggie in, followed by the other rescuers.

Sherry motioned to the examination table. "Bring him over here." Auggie moaned softly as Mr. Otto gently laid him down.

"I'll get the doctor," Sherry said.

Hearing the commotion, Dr. David Elf was already on his way and met Sherry in the hall. They hurried back into the room and Dr. Dave proceeded to Auggie's side. He removed the blanket and quickly felt Auggie's limbs and body, noticing his icy clothing. Then he raised Auggie's eyelids and looked into his eyes.

"Good, there's no apparent injury." He turned to Mr. Otto. "You may want to call Santa and bring him up to date. There's a phone at the nursing station. The rest of you will have to go to the waiting room."

"Yes, sir," Mr. Otto said. "Come on, fellows. Let's go."

Dr. Dave removed Auggie's now thawing clothes. He discovered that Auggie had an extra shirt and pair of pants on. That was good, for it probably prevented frostbite.

"Sherry, he said, "draw a tub of cold water. We must bring his temperature back up gradually."

"Yes, sir."

After putting Auggie in the tub, Dr. Dave said, "Would you go call the helicopter base and have them stand by? I'll continue monitoring Auggie. If he doesn't respond, he'll have to be hospitalized in Elfland."

As Sherry approached the nursing station, the phone was ringing.

"Infirmary."

"This is Santa. I didn't mean to pull you away from your duties, but I have a message for the rescuers."

"That's all right, Santa. I was coming to the phone to call the helicopter base and put them on notice."

"I anticipated that and they're already standing by," Santa said. "Please tell Mr. Otto and the rest of the elves to go to the dining hall. Mrs. Fineworthy is saving supper for them."

"Yes, sir."

"And Sherry, I have the greatest confidence in you and Dr. Dave. Augustus couldn't be in better hands."

"Why, why thank you, sir. We'll keep you posted as things develop."

"Please do. Thank you, Sherry."

"Good-by, sir."

Sherry relayed Santa's message to the rescuers and told them they could come back after they ate supper. Then she returned to assist Dr. Dave. The other elves got up to leave, but Tater remained seated.

"Come on Tater, let's go," Robbie said.

"No. I-I'm staying here."

"But Tater, we missed lunch. You must eat; it's a long time until breakfast."

"I'm not hungry. Besides, I don't feel very good."

"I hope you're not coming down with something. Maybe Dr. Dave should check you later."

"No, it's nothing like that," Tater insisted. "I'll be all right."

Robbie left, shaking his head in confusion. It wasn't like Tater to miss a meal.

In the infirmary, Sherry and Dr. Dave were gradually adding more warm water. Color began returning to Auggie. His lips, hands, and feet were becoming bright red, and Auggie was moaning softly and moving a little.

"The circulation is picking up now," Dr. Dave pointed out. "He will experience some pain, but that's a good sign. I believe we can move him to a room before long."

"I'll go prepare one," Sherry said.

Out in the waiting room, the rescuers were returning. Robbie handed Tater a lunch sack.

"I thought you might need this."

Tater thanked Robbie and placed it on the chair beside him.

The elves were tired and anxious as they waited. At one point, Mr. Otto led them in prayer; but for the most part they were quiet. Each one was lost in his own thoughts - each one was pulling for Auggie in his own way.

Dr. Dave and Sherry moved Auggie to a room, put him to bed and covered him with blankets. Periodically they checked his vital signs. Finally, Dr. Dave raised up after examining Auggie.

"He's one tough little customer. I think he'll be all right now."

Sherry blinked back tears. "I must tell the others."

"Fine - you do that, and I'll go call Santa."

Sherry went to the waiting room. As she entered, all eyes were upon her.

"He's going to make it," she announced.

"Thank goodness!" Mr. Otto exclaimed. The rest of the elves let out a collective sigh of joy and relief.

"Now," Sherry said, "I want all of you to go to your bunkhouses and get a good night's sleep. You have done your job well, and you're exhausted. Dr. Dave and I will take turns monitoring Auggie through the night. We'll update you at breakfast in the dining hall."

After saying goodnight to Sherry, the elves left. Only Tater lingered behind. Sherry turned and looked at him questioningly.

"Sherry, may I please see Auggie?"

"That's not possible right now, Tater. He's resting."

"Oh, please, Sherry! Just for a moment . . . I - I - must talk to him."

"He probably wouldn't even know you were there, Tater."

"It doesn't matter. I just have to see him," he begged.

Sherry looked into his pleading eyes and sighed. "All right, just for a moment. And if Dr. Dave comes back, you make yourself scarce. Auggie's in room #2."

"Oh, thank you, Sherry!" And off he went.

Entering the dimly lit room, he eased over beside Auggie and whispered, "Auggie, Auggie, do you hear me? This is Tater . . ." No response.

It was so quiet, he could hear Auggie's shallow breathing. Maybe this wasn't such a good idea after all. Auggie probably wouldn't hear him anyway, but there was something on his conscience, and Tater had to get it off. He reached down and took Auggie's hand in his. "Auggie, there's something I must tell you. Something very bad. While you were lying out there in the cold . . . I - I ate your piece of pie you left in the truck. I didn't mean to . . . I, I couldn't help it. I was just going to eat a little bit . . ." his voice trailed away. Not knowing if Auggie heard him or not, Tater continued, "I'm sorry, Auggie. Please forgive me."

He gave Auggie's hand a squeeze and started to leave, but wait - what was that? There - there it was again. No mistake! Auggie had weakly squeezed back.

"Oh, Auggie," Tater exclaimed, "the next time we have pie, you can have my piece!" Out the door he eased and went scurrying down the hall.

"Thanks," he flung gleefully over his shoulder to Sherry as he passed by. She looked rather bewildered. When he got to the front door, Tater suddenly skidded to a stop. He turned and looked back up the hall and spied the lunch sack.

"Oh, no," he said, rubbing his belly, "can't forget that. BOY, AM I HUNGRY!"

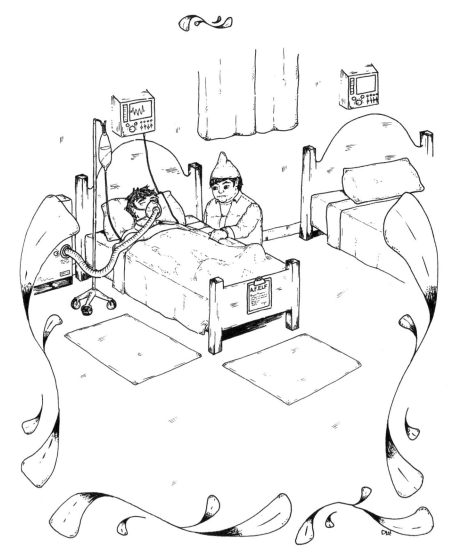

A Soulful Confession

Chapter 9

Recovery

The dining hall was abuzz the next morning when Robbie set his tray down and took a seat at the table with Mandy, Tater, and Pam.

"Has Sherry come in?" he asked.

"Yes," Mandy replied. "She's reporting to the foremen now."

Robbie looked around at the platform and saw Sherry coming toward them.

"Here she comes now."

As Sherry took her seat, Mr. Otto stood up and rapped on the table with his spoon. "Your attention. Your attention, please!" Everyone got quiet. "As most of you know by now, we found Augustus late yesterday afternoon, and his condition was poor. However, with the help of Dr. Dave, Sherry, and all your prayers, it looks like he will be just fine. Sherry reported to us this morning that he had a rough night, but is now resting comfortably and taking some nourishment."

There was a chorus of yeas and applause and Mr. Otto tapped the table again.

"There will be no visitors allowed today. He needs rest and time to recover."

There was joy in the dining hall this morning. Mr. Otto could see it, especially in the faces of Robbie, Sherry, Pam, Tater, Mandy - and yes, he was smiling, too.

Later that morning up at the barn Mr. Olaf had finished his normal chores and decided it was time to begin getting Santa's sleigh ready for his long journey. There was something magical about that sleigh, for there was no telling how many miles it traveled each year. Yet, it only took a little cleaning and dusting before it looked brand new again. Of course, there were the reins to repair and all the silver bells and accessories to clean and polish. All in all, it was quite a chore, especially for an old elf like himself. Yes, he would start a little earlier this year.

The first thing Mr. Olaf did was put a heater in the tack room. Then he swept and mopped the floor. He liked to keep things neat and clean, just like in the barn. Even though the barn was getting old, everyone said he kept it immaculate.

He went over and was folding up the canvas cover on the sleigh when he saw a flashlight on its floor. Reaching down, he saw something else and picked it up.

A letter.

The envelope was smeared and dirty, but the letter inside seemed to be intact.

Must belong to that young fellow who spent the night here, he said to himself. Bet he sure was cold. Too bad I didn't start working out here yesterday. If I had, he could have used the heater. He's lucky they found him in time. "I'll drop these by the infirmary," he muttered, and laid them on his workbench.

Then he went over to a big wooden box, opened the lid, and

began taking out the harness and spreading it - one section at a time - along the floor. After he finished laying the last piece out in its proper place, he walked along slowly inspecting it.

"Oh, my," he said, "they're really in bad shape this year."

Mr. Olaf heard Santa Claus calling to him. "In here, Santa."

"Oh, there you are," Santa said, as he entered the tack room.

They discussed Donner's injury and Santa seemed most pleased with the progress. He looked down at the harness and accessories spread over the floor.

"Looks like you have a lot of work there."

"Yes, sir, I agree."

"The toy factories are working at peak performance now Mr. Olaf, and in a few more days they should be caught up in production. Perhaps we can spare someone to give you a hand then."

"No - no, Santa, that won't be necessary. I can still manage."

"Oh, of course you can," Santa laughed. "I didn't mean you couldn't handle all of your chores. It's just that the carpenters and I will be taking a lot of your time drawing up plans for the new barn."

"In that case," Mr. Olaf said with a smile, "I guess I could use a little help."

"Good." Santa looked at his watch. "I'd better be off. I have a meeting with the plant foremen this morning, and if I hurry, I can go by the infirmary and check on Augustus." He turned to leave.

"Wait!" Mr. Olaf picked up the flashlight and letter and handed them to Santa. "If you're going by the infirmary, you can save me the trip. I found these in the sleigh and assume they belong to that young fellow."

"I'll be glad to drop them off," Santa said, and put them in his coat pocket.

On his way to the infirmary, Santa had a lot of things on his mind. Mr. Olaf was one of them. With all of his experience and love of the reindeer, he would be a hard man to replace. Well, at least he was staying on over the summer to oversee the building of the new barn. He would put an ad in the monthly edition of the North Pole Newsletter after Christmas in hopes of finding a qualified replacement. With this and many other things on his agenda, Santa forgot to leave the letter and flashlight at the infirmary. After his meeting with the plant foremen, he returned home.

Mother Claus, hearing Santa come in, said in a loud voice from the kitchen, "I'm glad you're back, dear. Wash up, lunch is almost ready."

"Right away."

He was hanging up his coat when he saw the flashlight protruding from the pocket. He took it out with the letter. I'll return these tomorrow, he thought.

"Hurry, dear," Mrs. Claus called.

Walking through the kitchen, he laid the letter and flashlight on the counter, leaned over and gave Mother Claus a peck on the cheek.

"I don't know what I'd do without you," he said on his way to wash up.

After lunch Santa went into his office to attend to a mass of paper work while Mother Claus cleaned up the kitchen. She washed the dishes, put them away, and had begun wiping off the counter when she came across the flashlight and the letter.

She took the letter out of the envelope and read it. Puzzled, she took it into Santa.

"This letter was on the counter."

"Oh, yes," Santa said. "Mr. Olaf found it in the sleigh this morning and I meant to drop it off at the infirmary for Augustus."

"You mean this Augustus is the same one you were sending home?"

"I'm afraid so!"

"Oh, dear," Mrs. Claus said. "No wonder he didn't want to go home. The envelope was smudged and I thought it was one of our letters that you'd left on the counter for me to read. I picked it up and read it by mistake. Now I'm very concerned Santa, and I think you should read it, too."

"Well, then, by all means let me see it."

Santa slipped on his reading glasses and looked at the letter. "'Oh, dear' is right," he said.

"Is there any way at all that he can stay?" she asked.

"I had an idea this morning, but I'll have to check it out with Mr. Olaf; then we'll only have one problem to solve."

"What could that be?"

"Well," explained Santa, "if Augustus disobeyed and intentionally missed the helicopter, then he cannot stay."

"Oh, I see," she said. "If he intentionally disobeyed a valid order, then he must not be allowed to profit from it."

"That's correct."

"How will you find out?"

"Oh, that's the easy part. I'll just ask him, for as you know, elves do not lie."

"Of course," Mrs. Claus said, "but how could he have missed the helicopter?"

"You don't know Augustus very well," Santa said, shaking his head. "The funny part of all this is that this morning I talked to Mr. Olaf, and mentioned sending someone from the factories to help him out due to his additional duties. Then after the meeting with the plant foremen, I find that the demand is up and our quota had to be raised. The fact is, I really do need Augustus."

"Then, if he somehow accidentally missed the helicopter, can he stay?" she asked anxiously.

"If Mr. Olaf and Augustus are agreeable, we may be able to keep him. The hard part will be trying to find a place for him to stay. As you know, all the bunkhouses are full."

"Oh, Santa, try to work it out."

Santa hesitated for a moment. "First things first, my dear, but I'm thinking on it."

The next morning, Santa went to the infirmary to see Dr. Dave and check on Auggie's condition.

"Oh, he's doing fine," Dr. Dave said. "As a matter of fact, we will have him up and around today."

"Very good. Will it be alright if I go in and see him, then?"

"Certainly, sir."

"Thank you."

Santa entered the room just as Sherry was removing Auggie's breakfast dishes.

"Good morning, Sherry . . . Augustus."

"Good morning," they both answered, and Sherry excused herself and left the room, closing the door behind her.

"Dr. Dave tells me you're doing very well."

"Yes, sir; I feel fine."

"Good," Santa said. "Augustus, I need to discuss some things with you."

"I was afraid of that," Auggie said, swallowing hard.

"Now, Augustus, just relax. I only have a few questions to ask you."

"Yes, sir."

"First of all, we have just about figured out what you did after missing the helicopter, but now I need to know why you missed your flight."

Auggie took a deep breath.

"Well, sir, after leaving the post office, I saw them unloading the helicopter and putting supplies into the supply truck. The wind was cold and I decided to step around to the other side of the post office and wait for them to deliver the supplies and come back. But for some reason, the truck never came by and the next thing I knew, the helicopter was revving the engines for take off."

"Then you didn't purposely miss the helicopter?"

"Oh, no, sir. I chased after it yelling to them, but they didn't see or hear me."

"I see," Santa said. "Then why didn't you report to me after missing your flight?"

Auggie dropped his head. "I didn't want to cause you any more trouble, sir. I-I was so embarrassed and ashamed. I thought after everyone went to bed, I could hide in the barn and board the helicopter when it came back without anyone knowing. It was a poor decision sir, and I'm sorry for all the trouble I caused everyone."

Santa listened attentively, occasionally rubbing his beard.

Then he said, "The main thing, Augustus, is that you were found in time and you're going to be all right." He reached into his coat pocket and took out the letter and flashlight. "Mr. Olaf found these in the sleigh and asked me to return them to you."

"Thank you, sir."

"I'll be back to see you tomorrow." Then Santa left and went directly to the barn.

Santa explained to Mr. Olaf what he had in mind. Mr. Olaf nodded his head in agreement and they walked over to the tack room. They both studied it carefully.

"It could be possible with a little work," Mr. Olaf said.

"That's what I thought. You'll need some help and I have two volunteers in mind."

"It shouldn't take but a day," Mr. Olaf surmised. "I'll get the supplies together."

"Good," Santa replied. "I'll send your volunteers to you in the morning."

Chapter 10

A New Beginning

The day was a busy one for Auggie. After breakfast he went for a walk in the halls of the infirmary and at one point he'd even stood outside for a few minutes in his robe. It felt good to be up and around.

During lunch, Mr. Otto came by with all of the rescuers and Auggie thanked each one of them. Mr. Otto told him how everyone in the dining hall had volunteered to help in the search. Auggie was amazed that he'd caused so much concern.

"After all, this is the North Pole," Mr. Otto had said. "Up here, we're just one big family."

That evening after supper, Pam, Mandy, Tater and Robbie came by for a visit and Sherry joined them. They spent the evening talking, joking and reminiscing about the good times - the Sundays after lunch at the dining hall when almost everyone spent the afternoons playing games, trying out the new toys, or just relaxing with friends after a week of hard work. Santa and Mrs. Claus would come for supper and afterwards they would pull Mrs. Fineworthy's piano out by the big stone fireplace. Then, to the sounds of the piano, and the crackling of the fire, they would sing songs until late in the evening. And like those evenings, this one - all too soon - came to an end.

Now, lying awake in his bed, Auggie thought about them. What a good group of friends they were; he would miss them very much. Auggie realized his time was running out. He had recovered and soon would be released from the infirmary and there was only one place to go . . . that was home!

The next morning he had another visitor. It was Larry from the laundry. They had cleaned and pressed all his clothes and Larry had brought them over to him. Auggie thanked him.

Then Larry said, "Auggie, there's one problem."

"What's that?"

"Well, your hat wouldn't come out right, no matter what we did. I guess it froze in place when you slept on it."

"Let's see," Auggie said, and tried it on while Larry held a mirror for him. Sure enough, the hat fell to one side instead of backward. Auggie pushed it back, but each time it just fell to one side.

"I see what you mean," Auggie agreed.

"We looked for you another one but we didn't have any your size. We should have some within a day or two. If you like, I'll bring you a new one."

"No, this is just fine. Maybe it'll remind me to stay out of trouble."

Auggie thanked him again, and Larry left.

A few minutes later, Dr. Dave came in.

"Augustus, you're as fit as a fiddle and I'm releasing you today."

Auggie bit his lip.

"You may go to the dining hall for lunch, but return to the infirmary afterwards, because Santa has called and is planning to come by for you later."

After Dr. Dave left, Auggie walked over to the window and stood for a long moment looking out over the compound.

Well, this is it, he thought.

Around noon, Sherry came by to see if he would join them for lunch at the dining hall now that he was released. He had diplomatically declined saying that he wasn't hungry, which he wasn't. But Auggie had already made up his mind, for Santa would be coming soon to send him home and he wanted to remember his friends the way they were last night - laughing and happy, not in tearful good-byes in the dining hall.

At 1:30 p.m., he decided to go to the office and wait for Santa. He picked up his things and headed for the office. Going up the hall, he passed by the linen room. Sherry was inside with her back to him, folding sheets. He stopped in the doorway for a moment. She'd always been especially kind to him and never laughed at any of the awkward things he did, not to mention the long hours she'd spent by his bedside until he was out of danger. He started to speak, to say good-by; no, no, he wouldn't, but he would always remember her.

He entered the office and saw Santa was already there talking to Dr. Dave. Santa looked up.

"Oh, there you are, Augustus. I was just about to send for you. Are you ready to go?"

"Yes - yes sir," Auggie said, and he put on his hat and coat.

"Good, then let's be on our way."

Auggie thanked Dr. Dave and followed Santa out the door

and along the path until they came to the walkway. Then, a funny thing happened. Santa turned up the walkway and Auggie turned down the walkway toward the heliport. He took a few steps when he realized Santa was going in the opposite direction. Auggie turned and hurried to catch up. He was puzzled; why were they headed this way? Oh, yes, they were going to the bunkhouse to get his duffel bag. However, when they reached the bunkhouse, they went right on by. Santa must need to see Mr. Olaf, but would he not pick me up on the way back? Oh, well, I'll just have to wait and see. They tromped on.

Approaching the barn, they could hear hammering coming from the tack room. Mr. Olaf was outside taking a mattress from the supply sleigh. He looked up and motioned for them to follow him. They entered the tack room and saw that Mr. Olaf had the lid up on the big bridle box and was putting the mattress into it. Tater and Robbie were nailing up a frame for a small shower stall at the back of the room. They stopped and waved at Auggie. He waved back.

Santa walked over to Mr. Olaf.

"Looks like it's coming along very well - even better than I expected."

"Yes, sir. I managed to get everything I needed except a bed frame. We didn't have an extra one anywhere."

"I see." Santa pointed to the bridle box. "What are you doing there?"

"Well, sir," Mr. Olaf said, "I think this will work. Come here, Augustus. Climb in there and see how it feels."

This seemed odd to Auggie, but he immediately climbed in and stretched out.

"This feels just fine, sir."

"Could you be comfortable sleeping there?" Mr. Olaf asked.

"No problem, sir."

"Good," Mr. Olaf said. "Then we've solved the problem of your bed."

Auggie sat bolt upright. "My . . . my bed?" he stuttered, looking at Santa.

"Yes," Santa said. "Mr. Olaf has some additional duties this year and could use some extra help."

Tater, who along with Robbie had been listening intently, dropped his hammer which struck him right on his big toe. He let out a low howl of pain. "Ow-w-w-w-w!"

Auggie jumped out of the box and grabbed one of Santa's hands in both of his.

"Oh, thank you sir, thank you, sir!"

"You have Mr. Olaf to thank, too, for he agreed to take you on."

Auggie then shook Mr. Olaf's hand. "Thank you, too, sir. I'll do my best, I promise."

"I'm sure you'll do just fine, son," Mr. Olaf said. "Not everyone is cut out to work in a factory. Someday you'll find your niche in life, and when you do, you'll be a success."

Auggie turned toward Robbie and Tater who were grinning from ear to ear. He rushed toward them yelling, "I'm staying . . . I'm staying!" They grabbed each other's arms and started jumping up and down with glee, although Tater could only use one foot.

That evening at supper, Santa and Mrs. Claus were discussing Auggie.

"I'm so proud of you, Santa," she said.

"It's very pleasing when things work out to everyone's benefit," he answered with a smile.

A little later, while they were washing dishes, Santa confided, "By the way, dear. I learned a new word today."

"Oh?"

"Yes; you see, Mr. Otto is very fond of Augustus, so I dropped by and informed him of my decision. He was pleased and said that at least if he commits an 'Auggieism' up at the barn, he won't stop production."

"An 'Auggieism'?" Mother Claus asked.

"Yes, now-a-days, that's what the fellows at Plant #3 call a goof-up."

"Oh, Santa!" she exclaimed, and they both laughed out loud.

The next few weeks passed quickly for everyone at the North Pole, especially Auggie. The factories were running overtime at full production, and Auggie and Mr. Olaf were quite busy themselves.

At first Auggie started his new job doing menial tasks, like cleaning the barn, and feeding and brushing down the reindeer. Mr. Olaf found time each day to teach and instruct him on the responsibilities of keeping the barn, and in the nature and care of reindeer.

"These are very special animals," Mr. Olaf said. "They need very special care."

Auggie really didn't know how extraordinary they were until one afternoon when Mr. Olaf let him tag along while he took the reindeer out for their daily exercise. They put on their snowshoes and trekked along a path that took them to a big barren valley about two miles from the compound. The reindeer were eager, and occasionally Mr. Olaf would firmly but gently tell them to calm down and not get too far ahead of Auggie and himself.

When they reached the valley, they stopped.

"Auggie, you are about to see something fantastic," Mr. Olaf said, "something that few people have ever seen."

The reindeer were pawing the ground in anticipation, so Mr. Olaf walked up to the front and gave Rudolph a pat on the shoulder. "OK boy, now go!"

Mr. Olaf was right. Auggie was absolutely astonished at the things they did. He knew that Santa's reindeer were unique, but he'd never imagined how remarkable they were. Auggie decided then and there that he was going to learn all he could about these magnificent creatures. He soon found out that they were very sensitive and playful, too.

One evening, after exercise, Auggie was standing on his stool brushing down Vixon, when he apparently brushed her too hard. She bumped him off the stool, stamped her foot, and glared down at him.

In the beginning, Auggie felt that the reindeer only tolerated him, for they were used to Mr. Olaf's gentle touch and ways. He was sure that they wondered who this new intruder was, and only accepted him because of Mr. Olaf. Even so, as the days passed, they grew accustomed to him and he felt that they were even amused sometimes at his awkward ways.

One morning Auggie was up in the loft breaking open bales of hay. He used the pitchfork to toss the hay down a chute to the floor below so he could feed the reindeer. The work wasn't hard, but he got an idea how to do it easier. He pulled a bale of hay over to the chute and untied the strings holding it together. He put down the pitchfork. This is easier he thought, as he bent over and gave the bale a big push. But . . . to his surprise, the bale came apart in his hands and he fell head first down the chute. Auggie let out a yell as he hit into the pile at the bottom with the rest of the bale coming down on top of him.

After he realized the only thing that he hurt was his pride, he pushed the hay off and started to get up. That's when he heard the reindeer noises. He looked up. They were all around him and he knew they were laughing at him. At first he was flustered and as he tried to get up, Prancer tipped him back over with his nose; then Dasher, then Blitzen. Each time Auggie tried to get to his feet, one of them would playfully knock him over into the hay. They were stamping their feet, and tossing their heads. Before long, Auggie's frustration turned into uncontrollable laughter.

Mr. Olaf, upon hearing all the commotion, stepped out of his office, watched for a few moments, and said, "Augustus, when you get through playing with the reindeer, please continue with your chores."

After that, the reindeer would come up and nuzzle Auggie sometimes and he would pet them. He felt good because he knew they had finally accepted him.

By this time, Auggie's chores had been expanded; his hard work and willingness to learn had earned Mr. Olaf's confidence. Auggie was also experiencing a new and different feeling . . . one that he was unaccustomed to . . . for he almost felt like - like here was a place where he finally fit in.

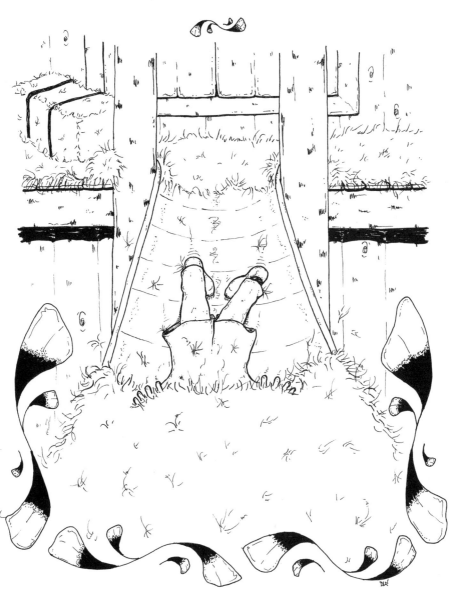

OOPS!

Chapter II

A Day Off

It was three days until Christmas and Santa had made his rounds of the plants. Production was coming to an end. In fact, Plant #7 would finish today and begin its clean up operations. Everything was coming together on schedule.

Santa went by the barn and checked in with Mr. Olaf. The sleigh was ready and the reindeer were rested and healthy. He was pleased and very proud of everyone.

It was a big year in terms of production and he knew how tired they all must be. He, too, was nearly exhausted but in a good mood. It would be nice to have a couple of days rest before he made his great journey. When Santa entered his house, he was chuckling to himself. He continued to do so as he hung up his coat. Mother Claus was sitting by the window knitting a Christmas gift.

"What's so funny, dear?" she asked.

Santa tried to suppress his laughter.

"After going by the plants, I went up to the barn. When I entered, Mr. Olaf was telling Augustus to carry the bridle reins to the tack room and put them on the sleigh because they were repaired and ready to go."

"What was so funny about that?"

"Well, my dear, no sooner had Mr. Olaf and I seated ourselves in the office than we heard Augustus cry out and then the sound of bells clattering. It was an awful ruckus so we rushed outside and found him all tangled up in the reins. Apparently he slipped on some ice, and as he tumbled over he became so entangled he couldn't get free. It was one of the funniest things I've ever seen."

"Oh, Santa, you shouldn't have laughed at him," Mother Claus scolded, but then burst into laughter herself.

"I didn't, dear. But I could hardly wait until I got back home so that I could."

"How is Augustus doing at the barn?" she asked, wiping her eyes. "Any more problems?"

"Oh, no, quite the contrary. He's doing an outstanding job according to Mr. Olaf. He's even expanded Augustus' chores to include taking the reindeer to exercise."

"That's a big responsibility."

"Yes, but that's not all." Santa smiled. "Augustus' personality hasn't changed, but his attitude has. He seems to have more confidence in himself now."

"How wonderful!"

"He's also been studying Mr. Olaf's veterinarian books so he can learn everything possible about the reindeer. You know, they seem to have a real affection for Augustus. Mr. Olaf says he doesn't know how he would've made it these past weeks without him."

"I'm so happy you found a way for him to stay," Mother Claus said, and smiled broadly.

"So am I, my dear, so am I."

The next day Auggie was doing his chores. Mr. Olaf stepped out of his office.

"Augustus, come here please."

Auggie walked over.

"Yes, Mr. Olaf?"

"How would you like an afternoon off?"

"Why, I hadn't thought of it, sir," Auggie said.

"Well, you haven't had much time for yourself since coming up here to work with me. You even have chores to do on Sunday."

"I don't mind, sir."

"I know, son," Mr. Olaf said, "but you've been a great help and you deserve an afternoon off. The factories are winding down so you may go visit your friends. Besides, I would like to spend some time with the reindeer."

"If you're sure, sir. I know you've been working hard on the plans for the new barn."

"Yes, Auggie, I have; and it saddens me in a way. I've spent a lot of years here in the barn, but like me, it's getting old and rickety - and we do need a new one. The plans can wait; now it's almost lunch time, so run along and take the rest of the day off. I'll exercise the reindeer and take care of the chores."

"I'll check in with you later, in case you need me, sir."

Mr. Olaf straightened himself. "Now see here young man, I'm perfectly capable of . . ."

"Hold it," Auggie cut in. " . . . of taking care of the barn without some whipper-snapper checking in on me," he mimicked and ran for the barn door laughing. He looked back and

Mr. Olaf was standing there smiling and shaking his head.

"That boy . . . that boy!"

Auggie saw his usual friends at the dining hall. Robbie pointed out two of the big people and told Auggie they were the helicopter pilots who helped search for him. Auggie went over, introduced himself and thanked them.

"Oh, we didn't do that much," Frank said.

"No," Joe added. "We were just glad to help out."

"I really wouldn't have minded riding in your helicopter," Auggie said, "but that's one flight I'm glad I missed."

"Maybe sometime during summer break when we're not busy, we'll take you up," Frank said.

"Really?! I'd like that; can my friends come?"

"Sure."

"Well, we have to be on our way," Joe said.

"There's another storm coming in this evening, so we must return to base."

They stood up to leave and Frank reached down and patted Auggie on the shoulder. "Little fellow, stay in out of the cold, you hear?" he said with a smile and winked at Auggie.

"Yes sir, you bet!" Auggie answered, and the pilots walked away.

He returned to the table and Robbie said, "Auggie, Plant #3 has finished production and they're starting clean up operations."

"Why don't you come back with us and visit Mr. Otto and the other fellows," Tater suggested.

"That sound great," Auggie said. "Let's go."

Auggie enjoyed his visit. He hadn't been back to the plant

since his last incident. He saw some of his former fellow workers and bunkmates and then he went to the office. He saw Mr. Otto through the window doing some paperwork. Auggie knocked on the door.

"Come in."

He went in and Mr. Otto looked up.

"Augustus, what a pleasant surprise! Have a seat. I haven't seen much of you lately."

"I've been pretty busy, sir."

"So I've heard, and doing very well Santa tells me."

"Thank you, sir," Auggie said, noticing that Mr. Otto was looking at his hat.

"Shouldn't you do something about that?" Mr. Otto remarked.

"Uh-huh," Auggie said. "Larry did inform me that the new ones were in, but I decided to keep this one."

"Why?"

"Well, sir, this hat is a little different now, like me, and when I put it on each morning, it reminds me to stay out of trouble."

"Well, it seems to be working." Mr. Otto smiled. "Oh Augustus, before you leave I would like for you to do me a favor."

"Anything, sir."

"Come with me then."

Auggie followed Mr. Otto over to the side of a big sewing machine. There was a bundle on the floor covered by a piece of plastic. Mr. Otto raised the cover and underneath was a roll of red carpet.

"This is the carpet they roll out for Santa in the dining hall each year. We have a big banquet when he returns from his great journey on Christmas Eve."

"I've heard about that banquet sir, and like the rest of the new elves, I'm really looking forward to it."

"Well, last fall Mr. Fineworthy brought this over to be cleaned and repaired, and I forgot all about it until the clean-up operations started."

"What you're telling me, sir, is that you committed an 'Auggieism'," Auggie said.

Mr. Otto's face turned red. "Then - then, you know?"

Auggie tried to fake a stern look, but couldn't hold it.

"Yes sir, I know," he giggled, "but it's something I can live with."

Mr. Otto shook his head and smiled. "Augustus, you just won't do."

They both laughed.

"Would you be kind enough to take this up to the dining hall and place it on the platform so Mr. Fineworthy will have it?" Mr. Otto asked.

"I'd be glad to, but if it's OK, I'll stay and help Robbie and Tater until supper time."

"That will be fine, Augustus, for I don't have to worry about your stopping production now, do I?" Mr. Otto walked away chuckling to himself.

That evening on the way to the dining hall, Auggie, Robbie, and Tater took turns carrying the carpet. Dark clouds were forming, a cold wind was beginning to stir, and snow was lightly falling.

"It looks like another storm is coming in," Tater said.

"Yes," Auggie agreed. "That's what Frank and Joe said."

After supper, he, Robbie, and Tater walked together to the bunkhouse. They asked him in, but Auggie declined and went on to the barn. Mr. Olaf was still there.

"Hi, Mr. Olaf. Thanks for the time off."

"Hi, Augustus. What are you doing back? I thought you would probably spend more time this evening with your friends."

"I would like that sir, but there's a storm coming in, and I thought I might borrow another one of your veterinarian books to study if that's all right?"

"Of course. Help yourself . . . anytime."

Auggie walked around the stalls and checked on each reindeer. Then he went into the office and selected a book. Mr. Olaf was there looking over some blueprints.

"I wouldn't stay too long, sir. The storm is getting worse."

"I'll keep that in mind. Good night, Augustus."

"Good night, sir."

But Mr. Olaf did work late, and when he left the barn, all the lights were out in the compound except the outside lights on each building.

Augustus was right. The storm was raging and the old barn was creaking in the fierce wind. He glanced over at the tack room and saw that Auggie's reading light was still on.

Making his way carefully down the walkway, Mr. Olaf smiled. He'd better do some reading himself or that young whipper-snapper would wind up knowing more about his job than he did.

Chapter 12

The Fire

The storm that swooped down on Santa's compound that night was not especially a vicious one. In fact, after a few hours it was diminishing, but it did have strong winds which had taken their toll on the old light fixture on the front of the barn. The arm that held the light was becoming unstable at its base and the screws were working loose in the deteriorated wood. Although the winds were subsiding, each gust pulled at it a little more. Finally it gave away, only to fall a few feet. There, it swung back and forth in the wind, suspended only by the electrical cords attached to it. Somehow the light still burned as it danced around in the swirling wind; but its weight, combined with the weight of the metal arm, was pulling heavily on the electrical wires. They strained and rubbed against the wood where they protruded from the barn. It wasn't long before the wires were getting hot and frayed. Finally, they broke, sending the light crashing to the ground as they snapped back into the barn spurting out a profusion of sparks that licked hungrily at the tender, dried out wood.

The sound of the light crashing down had startled the reindeer. They stood up and pawed around in their stalls for

Disaster Strikes

a few minutes before settling back down. It would be a while yet before they would smell the smoke.

Inside the tack room Auggie was sitting at his table, reading by the light of his small lamp. He stifled a yawn, stood up and stretched. It must be after midnight. He'd better get to bed. Even though the factories were winding down, he and Mr. Olaf still had plenty to do.

Auggie went over and turned down his bed, and noticed that the wind was quieter now.

"That's good," he said. "Maybe the storm has passed."

He walked over to the window to look outside. But before Auggie got to the window, he saw lights flickering across his room. Puzzled, he looked out and saw flames shooting out of the barn.

"OH - MERCY - NO!" he shouted, and he ran out the door donning his hat, coat, and mittens. He could hear the crackle of the flames. The heat made him step back as he unlatched the barn door and threw it open wide. Dancer, Prancer, and Blitzen rushed by him in a blur. Embers were falling and the smoke was so thick he could barely see the outline of the other reindeer.

He had to get them out, but first he must get help on the way. Auggie ran over to the big fire bell at the front of the barn and pulled the rope with all his might. BOING - BOING - BOING. The sound vibrated loudly down across the compound. He kept pulling the rope until he saw lights begin to come on. Then he ran back to the barn door and was met by Rudolph, who had managed to find his way out.

Auggie entered the barn. Smoke burned his eyes so he got

down low. The falling embers were starting more fires all around him. He knew the reindeer were frightened and disoriented, so he started calling out to them. Donner was close by and came to him. Auggie reached up and grabbed her ear and led her outside. Above the wind and crackling flames, he could hear the sounds of the fire brigade in the distance. Auggie gulped down fresh air and ran back into the barn. He repeated the process twice more.

The fire brigade and others were arriving when he went back in and caught Vixen. As the two neared the door, an ember bounced off Vixen's back. She reared up, knocking Auggie to the floor. He grabbed her leg and held on, talking to her until she calmed down. Stumbling, Auggie led her out, and then he fell on the ground gasping.

Members of the fire brigade hurried over and pulled him away from the barn. Sherry ran to his side and wrapped a blanket around him as he struggled to his knees and took in deep breaths of air.

"Are you all right?" Sherry asked.

Auggie was dizzy as he looked over at the reindeer. "Are they all out?" His vision was too blurred to count them.

Mr. Olaf, who was standing behind Auggie, said, "I'm afraid not, Augustus. Cupid is still missing, but there's nothing anyone can do."

Auggie got shakily to his feet and unsteadily made his way over to an elf holding a water hose. Before anyone realized what Auggie was doing, he stuck the blanket in front of the hose to get it wet, then flinging it over himself, ran stumbling toward the barn.

"AUGGIE! NO! STOP!" Sherry screamed.

"It's too late!" Mr. Olaf yelled, but Auggie had disappeared into the smoke and flames.

Mr. Olaf turned and saw Santa and Mrs. Claus had arrived with the elves who lived further down in the compound. He went over to them.

Fredrick, the fire chief, rushed up to report to Santa.

"It's a bad one, sir."

"Yes, I see," Santa replied with a grim face. "Is everyone safe?"

"I'm afraid not, sir. Mr. Olaf's new helper got all of the reindeer out, except Cupid."

"Where is Augustus?" Santa asked sadly. "I want to thank him."

"I'm sorry, sir, but before anyone could stop him, he went back in."

"Oh, dear!" Mrs. Claus exclaimed, staring in horror at the burning barn.

Inside the barn Auggie pulled the wet blanket over his head and looked vainly for Cupid. He didn't try to call out, for the smoke was choking him. With the roar of the flames, Cupid probably couldn't hear him anyway. Unable to find Cupid anywhere near the front of the barn, Auggie started making his way back to Cupid's stall, dodging flaming boards as they fell to the floor around him.

Nearing Cupid's stall, Auggie saw Cupid and the reason why she couldn't get out. A big smoldering beam had fallen across the front of the stall. Cupid was trapped. Auggie had to move the beam, and quickly, or both of them would perish.

Without hesitation, Auggie grabbed the beam. Steam came from his wet mittens, and they sizzled as he tugged as hard as he could. But he couldn't budge it - not an inch. Thinking quickly, Auggie felt his way over to the wall where the pitchfork hung. He got it and returned to the beam. His breath was coming in short gasps now, and his heart was pounding in his chest. The heat was nearly unbearable. This had to work. Time was running out. He wedged the pitchfork down beside the beam. Then with a mighty tug, Auggie felt it move. He tugged again and the beam fell away!

He entered the stall, and saw that Cupid was wide eyed and trembling. She was almost in shock. Auggie pulled the wet blanket off of himself and placed it over Cupid's head so she wouldn't be frightened by the flames. He talked softly and started leading Cupid out. He coughed and groped his way through the smoke. His eyes were burning and he felt tears streaming down his cheeks, but occasionally he could see spotlights shining through the door in order to help him find his way.

Outside, tension ran high. Everyone, including the reindeer, was staring at the barn door. Mrs. Claus knew it had only been a few minutes, but out here waiting - it seemed like an eternity. Mr. Olaf was standing beside her and Santa.

"He's been in there a long time sir," he said.

At that exact moment, the back part of the barn's roof swayed and then fell, sending sparks and flames shooting skyward.

Mrs. Claus clutched Santa's arm. "Is there any hope left?" she asked, her voice trembling.

"Yes, dear, but precious little, I'm afraid."

Suddenly someone yelled, "Look!" and a resounding chorus of cheers went up. Mrs. Claus jerked her head around toward the barn and couldn't believe her tear-filled eyes . . . for it was Auggie leading Cupid out of the burning barn!

Look! It's Auggie with Cupid!

The Fire

Chapter 13

Aftermath

Later that night, Auggie was taken to the infirmary where Dr. Dave treated his hands and bandaged them. Fortunately, the burns were only minor. Dr. Dave had Auggie stay at the infirmary so he could receive oxygen for a couple of hours to clear his lungs of smoke.

The next morning was a busy one for Auggie. First, Mr. Olaf came by.

"Hi, Auggie," he said. "I just came by to check on you and tell you that the reindeer are being kept in factory #7. We've set up temporary stalls and hay has been brought in. The reindeer are still very nervous and I hope they'll settle down and get some rest, for tomorrow night they have to make their great journey with Santa. It was a brave thing you did and we're all very proud of you, especially me, because these reindeer are like my children." He walked over to shake Auggie's hand but saw the bandages and patted Auggie on the shoulder instead. "I must get back to the reindeer." There were tears in the old man's eyes as he left the room.

Santa was Auggie's next visitor. While they were chatting, they heard a humming sound coming down the hallway. It got louder, and suddenly Ralph, the reporter for the North Pole

Newsletter, came scooting through the doorway in his motorized wheelchair. Santa jumped to one side out of the way.

"Oops! Good morning Santa," Ralph said sheepishly. "I'm sorry - I should be more careful."

"That's OK, come on in. I think this is the fellow you're probably looking for," Santa said, pointing to Auggie.

Santa stayed while Ralph interviewed Auggie, asking all sorts of questions like what town he was from, how long he'd been there, and so on.

Suddenly Ralph exclaimed, "Hey, you're the same elf that was being sent home, missed the helicopter, and got lost in the snowstorm. What a story!"

Santa frowned. "Er-Er, Ralph - hold on there. Don't you think the story of the fire is big enough?"

"Oh! I see your point. I guess I just get carried away sometimes." He took a picture of Auggie and Santa together. "By the way, Santa, do you want me to put your want ad for a stablemaster in this edition?"

"No . . . no, let's hold off on that for a while."

Soon after Santa and Ralph left, Auggie heard giggling out in the hallway. A moment later, Sherry, Pam, and Mandy came in with his lunch.

"Oh," Auggie said. "You didn't have to do that. I was coming to the dining hall."

"Oh, no you don't," Pam shushed. "Everyone wants to see you but we decided to keep you to ourselves."

The girls teased him and insisted on taking turns feeding him because his hands were bandaged. Auggie's protests were ignored. He felt uncomfortable with all this attention, but deep down inside he sort of liked it.

After the girls went back to work, Auggie left for factory #7 to join Mr. Olaf and the reindeer. Some of the equipment had been moved aside to make room for them. A makeshift corral and stalls had been set up with piles of hay on one side. Mr. Olaf was there alone and he explained that he wanted to keep the reindeer as quiet as possible.

Auggie walked into the corral and all the reindeer came up and nuzzled him. He petted each one and could sense their nervousness.

Around three o'clock that afternoon Mr. Olaf said, "Why don't we take the reindeer outside for a while. They haven't slept a wink, and maybe they can walk off some of their jitters."

"I think that's a good idea," Auggie agreed.

They led the reindeer out and down a back trail behind the factories. Mr. Olaf was careful to see that they didn't catch sight of the burned out remains of the barn.

When they returned, Mr. Olaf noted that it was supper time. "I think the reindeer will be all right while we go eat. All that walking has made me hungry."

"Oh, no sir," Auggie said. "You go ahead and bring me something back. I'll stay here."

"All right, Augustus. But there are a lot of people who would like to see you. Do I possibly detect that you're a reluctant hero?"

"Well . . . somewhat," Auggie admitted, "but mostly I'm still a little jumpy, too, like the reindeer. I'll go down for breakfast in the morning."

"I can certainly understand that, Augustus. I'll be back shortly."

Thirty minutes later Mr. Olaf returned with Auggie's supper. Auggie ate, and then even though his hands were sore, he helped Mr. Olaf brush down the reindeer. They took their time, petting and talking softly to each one.

After they finished, Auggie saw that - like himself - Mr. Olaf was tired and sleepy. A portable cot had been set up for Mr. Olaf, so he told Auggie to go on home and get some rest because tomorrow was a big day for them.

"I'd like to stay, too."

"But you don't have a cot to sleep on."

"That's OK," Auggie said, and pointed to a pile of hay he had spread out. "As tired as I am, that will do just fine."

Mr. Olaf chuckled. "Very well then, you may go on to bed. I'm going in the foreman's office and make a list of supplies we need."

Mr. Olaf finished his list and was getting ready for bed when he heard a soft tap on the door. He opened it and Santa came in.

"I thought I would check with you before calling it a night," Santa said. "How are the reindeer?"

Mr. Olaf put his fingers to his lips for quiet, and motioned for Santa to come look in the corral. There was Auggie, lying in the hay; and spread out around him in a semi-circle lay every one of the reindeer - and all were fast asleep.

"I see they are quite all right," Santa said.

"He has a way with them, sir."

"You've taught him well, Mr. Olaf."

"Well, I have to admit that at first I had some reservations."

"I, too, had reservations Mr. Olaf, but with Mrs. Claus' urging and your willingness to take responsibility for him, he turned out to be a 'God-send'. It just goes to show that when you go out of your way to help someone, you're generally repaid in kind. And I would have to say that young fellow has paid his debt in full!"

A Peaceful Sleep

Christmas Eve

The next morning Auggie was awakened by a tap on his foot.

"If you hurry, you can run take a shower and clean up before breakfast," Mr. Olaf said. "I'll wait here for you."

"Yes, sir." Auggie looked at the reindeer around him. No wonder he'd slept so warm. Comet and Dasher lay on each side of him and were beginning to awaken. Auggie arose and was quickly on his way to the nearby tack room.

He passed by the barn, and saw that the only thing left was the foundation. All the rest had been cleared away and disposed of. He wasn't surprised when he learned later that all of the elves who were not helping Mrs. Fineworthy decorate the dining hall for Christmas had volunteered to clean away the debris.

He took a quick shower and returned to factory #7. Then he and Mr. Olaf went to the dining hall. They had taken only a couple of steps inside when someone shouted, "There's Auggie!"

Everyone stood up and applauded. Auggie shuffled his feet and looked at Mr. Olaf.

"Do something," Mr. Olaf urged as the first wave of applause died down.

"Like what, sir?"

Mr. Olaf smiled at him. "You're a hero," he said, and reached down and took hold of Auggie's arm and raised it over Auggie's head like a victorious prizefighter.

The applause rose again.

Auggie tried to pull his arm down, but Mr. Olaf held it high for a long moment.

"Now you can go to your table," he said.

Auggie had just sat down at the table with his friends when they heard a familiar hum and the sound of feet sliding under tables. The aisle was not a safe place for feet and toes when Ralph was hot on a story. He wheeled up to their table and stopped.

"I thought you might like to see this," Ralph said, and laid down a copy of the North Pole Newsletter. On the front page were two pictures - one of Auggie as he came out of the burning barn with Cupid, and the one Ralph took of Auggie and Santa together. The big black headlines read: "DARING RESCUE SAVES REINDEER!"

Auggie swallowed hard and blushed. The next few minutes were ones he would never forget as different friends came over to congratulate him, including Mr. Otto. Even so, Auggie was happy when things settled back down. While they were eating breakfast, he noticed that the dining hall had a new look and mentioned it.

"Oh, yes," Sherry said. "A lot of us helped Mrs. Fineworthy while the rest cleared away what was left of the barn."

"It sure is beautiful," Auggie replied.

"We're all looking forward to the big banquet tomorrow evening when Santa returns," Robbie said.

"Yippee - all that food!" Tater exclaimed.

"Now, Tater," Pam warned, "Mrs. Fineworthy has you on a diet."

"I know, but I'll start after the banquet," he grinned, not realizing Mrs. Fineworthy had walked up behind him.

"You'll start right now," Mrs. Fineworthy insisted.

Tater froze with his fork in mid-air. She scooped up Tater's plate, which still had two biscuits on it, congratulated Auggie, and left.

Hot Off the Press

"Oh me," Tater moaned, "I'm going to starve!"

Everyone at the table laughed.

The rest of the day went by very quickly for Auggie and Mr. Olaf as they prepared the sleigh for Santa's big journey. Later that afternoon, they fed the reindeer special rations that Mr. Olaf prepared to sustain them on their trip. Around six o'clock that evening, Mr. Olaf decided it was time to put the harnesses on the reindeer.

"I thought we would do that after we eat," Auggie said.

"Oh no, Augustus. Santa leaves after supper and no one is allowed to see him pack all the gifts in the sleigh or see him depart. We all stay in the dining hall until after he's gone."

"Why is that?" Auggie asked.

"Augustus, there are a lot of mysteries at the North Pole, and only Santa knows the answers to all its secrets. I guess that's the way it's meant to be."

"Still, I'd like to know how he gets all those gifts into the sleigh."

"Ha, ha, ha," Mr. Olaf laughed. "In all the years I've spent here, not a Christmas has gone by that I didn't ask myself that same question."

The dining hall was abuzz with conversations that evening when Auggie entered. Most of the elves would get to go home over the New Year, and discussions of families and plans for the holidays were abundant. Others mentioned they were looking forward to the banquet and Santa's return when he would have gifts for all and tell them about his trip. Still, there was one conversation different from the rest. It was Tater, grumbling to himself as he looked at the meager portion of food Mrs. Fineworthy had allowed him.

Santa and Mrs. Claus had joined them for supper and were seated on the platform with the foremen. Now a tap-tap-tap came from that direction, and everyone looked. Santa stood up.

"Tonight represents what the North Pole is all about," he said, "love of mankind, peace on earth, and the joy of giving. Now I go to spread the bounty of your labor and that of many others to the children of the world!" He waved and started for the side door.

Auggie could feel the excitement as cheers broke out.

"Good luck, God speed, Bon Voyage," he and the others shouted. Then . . . Santa was gone.

The noise subsided and everyone was quiet, perhaps like himself, reflecting on the past year and their part in all of this, and experiencing a warm feeling deep inside. The distant sound of jingling bells penetrated the dining hall. The sound got closer and Auggie smiled. He'd polished those bells and now they would be heard all around the world. His chest filled with pride. Everyone was standing looking at the ceiling and listening intently.

Then they heard Santa say as he passed overhead, "HO-HO-HO - A Merry Christmas to all, and to all a good night!"

"Merry Christmas, Santa," Auggie whispered.

Chapter 14

Christmas at the North Pole

Almost everyone got to sleep late on Christmas Day. Auggie and Mr. Olaf were among those who didn't, because they had to clean the stalls and corral and prepare them for the return of Santa and the reindeer. They were bringing in fresh hay when Auggie stopped and looked up. "I thought they would be back by now."

"Oh, not so," Mr. Olaf replied.

"But I was taught that he only goes out on Christmas Eve, and now it's Christmas Day."

"That's true Augustus, but Santa starts out ahead of the sun, and as the earth turns, he continues to work in the darkness, which is Christmas Eve."

"Oh, I see. It's night in some part of the world at different times."

"I think you get the picture," Mr. Olaf said.

Auggie shook his head. "I still don't see how he does it!"

By eleven o'clock they had finished with their chores.

"Augustus, you can be off until this evening," Mr. Olaf said, "but when you hear the fire bells ringing, that's the signal that they have picked up Santa on radar and he'll be arriving soon. Then you report back here, for we have to take good care of the reindeer."

"OK," Auggie replied, and out the door he went toward bunkhouse #3 to find Robbie and Tater.

As he approached the bunkhouses, he saw a big snowball fight going on between houses #3 and #4. He rushed through the battleline to get to Robbie and Tater's side, and was relentlessly pelted. After about twenty minutes of furious snowballing, neither side seemed to be winning.

Suddenly someone on the other side shouted, "Hey, look! Let's get him!"

It was Mr. Otto coming up the walkway. He was still out of range as the bunkhouse #4 boys started throwing long range snowballs. Mr. Otto continued coming closer, seemingly unperturbed by the snowballs hitting around him.

While the other side was distracted, Auggie ran into the bunkhouse and soon returned with a broomstick. Tied to one end was a pillowcase. He raced to Mr. Otto's side and started waving it as he led him safely through the battle zone under a white flag of truce.

When they reached the other side Mr. Otto said, "Thanks, Augustus!" He turned back toward the combatants and gave a big sweeping mock bow. Everyone cut loose sending a barrage of snowballs raining down on the two of them. Mr. Otto scurried up the walkway out of range and they all howled with laughter. This seemed to take the steam out of the battle and it was soon called a draw.

Later, when they were going through the lunch line at the dining hall, Tater received some pleasant news.

Mrs. Fineworthy said, "Tater, during tonight's banquet you may eat as you please." His face lit up like a lightbulb.

"You've been doing good," she continued, "but you will be allowed only one small piece of apple pie. I hope you'll show some restraint."

While they were eating, Auggie noticed Tater kept glancing at him. "What is it, Tater?"

"I-er, I just remembered. I-um, owe you a piece of apple pie."

"That's OK," Auggie said, and smiled. "You may have it."

"Really?!" Tater's voice sounded like that of a drowning man who had just been thrown a life preserver. "Thanks, Auggie, you're a real pal!"

"Merry Christmas," Auggie replied, and they all laughed.

After they ate, Mandy suggested that they help clean up the kitchen because Mrs. Fineworthy's staff still had a lot of work to do before the banquet. Everyone at the table agreed.

That afternoon in the bunkhouse, Robbie was beating Auggie for the third straight time in a game of checkers when they heard the ringing of the fire bells.

"Santa's returning!" Robbie exclaimed.

"Saved by the bells," Auggie sighed and jumped up to go.

When Auggie reached Plant #7, Mr. Olaf was standing outside looking up into the sky.

"What are you looking at?" Auggie asked peering up into the darkness, seeing nothing.

"Santa"

"But they just picked him up on radar - hundreds of miles away."

"Sh-h-h . . . listen!"

Auggie heard the faint jingling of bells. Everyone standing outside cheered when Santa circled overhead. He landed beside his house and helped Mrs. Claus into the sleigh. Then he drove the reindeer at a trot through the compound while the elves hailed his return.

"Come," beckoned Mr. Olaf and they ran inside and opened the big service door. Santa, Mrs. Claus, and the reindeer entered. Mr. Olaf and Auggie closed the door behind them and approached Santa as he was helping Mrs. Claus down from the sleigh.

"Have a good trip, sir?" Mr. Olaf asked.

"Oh yes," Santa said, "but there is still unrest in some parts of the world. Hopefully, one Christmas Eve I'll be able to make my journey and see the whole world at peace."

"I hope so, sir."

While Santa and Mr. Olaf talked, Auggie was busy unhitching the reindeer. He could see they were tired and glad to see him. Auggie began leading them into the corral, and Santa came over to give each reindeer a few soft words and an affectionate pat.

Then he turned to Mr. Olaf and Auggie. "You fellows take good care of them; it was a long, hard trip. Afterwards please join us at the dining hall."

"Yes, sir," they replied in unison.

"And don't worry," Santa added as he winked at Mr. Olaf, "we won't start the festivities without you."

With that, Santa picked up his bag, put his arm around Mrs. Claus, and went out the door. Auggie could tell by the way Santa walked that he was very tired.

"Shouldn't Santa rest?"

"Probably," Mr. Olaf said, "but Santa looks forward to this banquet as much as the rest of us, and he wouldn't miss it for anything. You see, Augustus, tonight is our Christmas and also Santa's."

It took Auggie and Mr. Olaf a little over an hour to brush, feed, and bed down the reindeer. Once they were resting comfortably, Auggie and Mr. Olaf left for the dining hall.

The dining hall was alive with festivities when they entered. Christmas carols were being sung, and elves were going from table to table laughing and talking. The tables had been arranged to face the platform where a great buffet ran almost all the way across loaded with Mrs. Fineworthy's best creations. A podium was set to one side, and Santa's and Mrs. Claus' place of honor was close by. The entire room was beautifully decorated.

Mr. Olaf went to report to Santa and Auggie got himself some punch and assorted goodies at one of the hors d'oeuvres tables. Then he searched out Robbie, Tater, Pam, Sherry and Mandy, who were saving him a seat.

"Oh, this is a good one," Auggie said. "How'd you get a table on the front row?"

"We came in right after Santa landed," Pam answered.

They talked for a few minutes, then Santa stood up and everyone got quiet. He walked over to the podium.

"I see everyone is here now, so I'll begin with the highlights of my trip," he said.

Everyone listened attentively and "oohed" and "aahed" and occasionally laughed as he unfolded his latest journey out among the big people. This was a world that most of the elves had never seen, and the way Santa told his story made it seem like you were riding beside him in the sleigh.

Next he thanked all the elves for their part and their efforts for the cause of Christmas. "Although all of you are to be commended, there is one among you who took love and dedication further than anyone expected. Without his selflessness and courageous actions, this Christmas would have been the saddest in the history of the North Pole. Instead, it is one of our merriest. Ladies and gentlemen, I give you the elf that truly saved this Christmas, and soon to be the new stablemaster of the North Pole, AUGUSTUS F. ELF! Would you come to the podium please, Augustus?"

Auggie felt like he'd been hit with a giant snowball. "Stablemaster?" he mumbled.

Sherry nudged him in the side. "The podium. Go to the podium!"

"Uh . . . all right." He got shakily to his feet on weak knees and made his way up the steps and over beside Santa.

Everyone stood, cheered, and applauded.

"Stablemaster?" Auggie said to Santa. "But I'm not qualified. There's so much I don't know."

"You will be qualified, Augustus," Santa assured him. "Mr. Olaf is going to stay on and teach you until you're ready." Then Santa raised his arms for quiet and everyone settled back into their seats.

Mrs. Claus brought a tray to the podium that had a small box on it. Santa opened the box, took out a medal, and stepped behind Auggie.

"Augustus F. Elf," he said, hanging the medal around Auggie's neck, "We are honoring you with our very highest award. You are now, and throughout history will forever be, a Hero of the North Pole."

A Much Deserved Award

The whole dining hall exploded in applause and approval. Auggie stood there feeling a worthiness deep down inside like he'd never known or hoped to have. He was shaking and smiling at the same time. He felt an arm go around him. It was Mother Claus and she gave him a big hug. Mr. Otto, Mr. Olaf, and others were reaching up to the platform to shake his hand. Ralph was popping flashbulbs and taking pictures. Through all of this, Auggie could see his friends, especially Sherry, looking up at him with pride in their eyes. This was the greatest moment of his life!

Things finally settled back down and Santa said, "Augustus, Mrs. Fineworthy has outdone herself this time, and I'm sure the smell of this food has made us all hungry by now. So, you will have the honor of being first in line. Mr. Fineworthy, would you roll out the red carpet, please?"

Mrs. Fineworthy led Auggie over to the serving line. He picked up his tray and silverware, and started down the line. He didn't see the missing marble which had been concealed in the carpet all these months. The instant he stepped down on it, his feet shot out from under him and he hit with a crash. His silverware and tray went clattering upon the floor.

Auggie sat there and could feel the old embarrassment of being clumsy coming over him - then suddenly, he started laughing. It was contagious and everyone joined in. He couldn't help but laugh, for here he was . . . Hero of the North Pole and soon to be stablemaster . . . but he was still Auggie, the Awkward Elf. And you know what, he thought, IT'S OK TO BE ME!

Biographical Information

Author: Stacy A. Powell

Stacy is a poet, writer, and story-teller. He was born in Clifton, South Carolina, a small mill village just outside of Spartanburg. He joined the armed forces in his late teens and spent several years overseas. After fulfilling his military obligations, he continued to travel extensively on his own.

Somewhere along the way, an old longing to write caught up with him. Coming back to his hometown, he joined the Writer's Guild of Greenville, and eventually served for two years as the organization's president.

Co-Writer: Diane Fuller

Diane Fuller's hometown is Camden, South Carolina. She is the mother of a son and daughter, and has been employed at Wofford College in Spartanburg, South Carolina, for the last 17 years. While at Wofford, she has worked both as an editorial assistant and a human resources specialist.

Illustrator: Dan Nagro

Dan Nagro is a self-taught artist. He lives with his wife and two children in Spartanburg, South Carolina. This is his first illustration of a book, and Dan looks forward to a future in art.

Order Form for
The Legend of
Auggie the Awkward Elf

To order *The Legend of Auggie the Awkward Elf*, please send this order form together with your check or money order, include the price of the book and add $2.25 for the first book and $1.00 for each additional book for handling and mailing to:

CANDLE FLY PRESS
P.O. BOX 4561
SPARTANBURG, SC 29305

I have enclosed $ _____ Check _____ or money order as payment in full. Please no COD's.

Name_____

Address_____

City _____

State _____ Zip _____

Thank you for your order
Please allow 1-2 weeks for delivery.